MW00477483

# Red Pen Redemption

## A Christmas Adventure

# Endorsements

Wow! Ebenezer Scrooge, meet Helen (Nellie) Bancroft, your modern-day, before-and-after counterpart. Her cringe-worthy life and decisions are told with fast pacing, smart dialogue, and keen plotting. The only thing slow about this novella is where you'll choose to pause, reflect, and perhaps look in a mirror. It's a fun and poignant read and the perfect Christmas story for any season, reminding us of the redemptive power of God's saving grace through Jesus. I was left wanting both more of Ms. Roeleveld's writing (there are many stories left in this author I can tell) and a "flipping Bible" (you've got to read it to understand that one!) Would make a terrific gift too!

—**D.L.Koontz**, author of the *Crossing into the Mystic Series*

I couldn't turn the pages fast enough. *Red Pen Redemption* is a skillfully woven tale of one woman's life. All of it. The good, the beautiful, the painful, the ugly. When the final page is written, will her good outweigh the bad? And if not, will she accept the unrelenting grace that continues to pursue her? Combining solid theology with masterful storytelling, Lori Roeleveld has written a modern day parable that will inspire, encourage, and convict everyone who reads it.

—**Lynn Huggins Blackburn**, author of *Covert Justice* (Love Inspired Suspense)

Reading *Red Pen Redemption* is like opening a special gift on Christmas morning. Everything about this book delivers—from an engaging story to characters who are more like friends than people on a page. It takes place in a setting that begs one to visit it in person. Author Lori Roeleveld has moved to the top of my favorite writer list.

—**Edie Melson**, author of *While My Soldier Serves*

In *Red Pen Redemption*, Lori Roeleveld has crafted a brilliant re-imagining of Dickens' *A Christmas Carol*. It is a story that is at once familiar and new—one that will live on in the minds of the reader for years to come. Roeleveld creates characters that are tangible and real. Nellie's magical Christmas night is no less bizarre than the one Ebenezer Scrooge faces, but her process of self-discovery is both poignant and original; one rife with symbolism and the fresh perspective Roeleveld's readers have come to expect from her work.

—**Aaron Gansky**, author of *Hand of Adonai Series* and *The Bargain*

# Red Pen Redemption

## A Christmas Adventure

## Lori Stanley Roeleveld

# Elk Lake Publishing

Red Pen Redemption: A Christmas Adventure

Copyright © 2015 by Lori Stanley Roeleveld

Requests for information should be addressed to:
Elk Lake Publishing, Atlanta, GA 30024

ISBN-13 Number: 978-1-942513-71-1

Graphics Design: Anna M. O'Brien

Editor: Deb Haggerty

# Dedication

For Rob,
my partner in this Jesus adventure.
You're the Charles to my Helen.
Love always,
Me

# Acknowledgments

Writing appears to be a lonely venture, but entire teams carry each book across the finish line.

*Thank you* to Rob and my mom for doing all the things so I could write. Thanks to Dad for funding many meals out and to Hannah for never letting me quit. Thanks, Zack, for picking my spirits up when they fall.

*Thank you* to the team at Elk Lake Publishing, especially Deb Haggerty, who believed in this story from the start and made it shine.

*Thank you* to Becky Gansky, who encouraged me not to give up on Helen Bancroft. Thank you to all the readers who fell in love with the early versions of Red Pen Redemption. And thank you to the Prayer is the Work team who have prayed, are praying, and will continue to pray for those who read this book.

I am always grateful to share this writing adventure with the fine women of the Light Brigade, writing light into a dark world.

*Thank you*, Mickey, for the meals. Thank you, Les Stobbe, agent extraordinaire, and Rita, who keeps him on his toes.

This book is for all my friends who pray for and witness to aging parents who have yet to believe. Be diligent in prayer, persistent in hope, and lavish with love. Nothing done in the name of Jesus is done in vain.

# Chapter 1

"You didn't pull stunts like this when Dad was alive. You attended Christmas Eve services with him, why not with me?" Helen's grown daughter, Kat, stood in the doorway to Helen's study, beating her husband Paul's winter coat with a lint brush, attacking every one of Gatsby's Siamese hairs.

Helen glared over her reading glasses. "I warned Paul not to leave his Burberry lying on that chair. It's Gatsby's sunny nap spot from two to four."

Her favorite grandson, Harry, home from college, slid into the room sideways, squeezing past his mother as he poked at one of those hand-held computer gizmos. "Yeah, Gran. Come with us. It might be fun to see lightning strike the sanctuary when you darken the threshold! Muah-ha-ha-ha." He waved one hand around like Vincent Price in an old horror film then high-fived her as they shared conspiratorial smiles.

Kat scowled. "Not helping."

Harry ignored his mother. He balanced on the arm of the divan until Helen redirected him with one raised eyebrow to sit properly on the cushion. She scanned his lanky frame taking in the brown slacks, caramel button-down, and matching tie, all a lovely complement to his chestnut eyes and auburn hair. The spitting image of his grandfather. As he caught her critiquing, Harry raised a pant leg revealing lime green socks sequined with red Christmas trees. He grinned and winked.

"You're incorrigible!" she said as Harry recovered his garish sock before Kat discovered his secret.

Harry tapped his gadget again and nodded at Helen. "What are you doing up here alone anyway?"

"It's called reading, darling. This is a book." She waved her worn first edition of Dickens' *A Christmas Carol*. "It doesn't light up or require charging and it only contains one story. Surely you've encountered books in a history course?" She ignored his eye roll. "Speaking of which, do you know your grades?"

Harry thumped his tablet. "Just checked. They're not posted yet."

"Posted?"

"On-line, mother," Kat said. "Professors post grades to a website, like an electronic bulletin board. You've dodged my question." Kat checked her reflection in the mantle mirror. Pulling up each cheek, she tortured herself seeing how she would look without crow's feet.

"Katherine! Stop fussing with your face. We Bancroft women do not alter ourselves. We age gracefully and accept the natural progression of life. Live well and your face reflects simple honest living."

"Prunes are simple and honest," Harry said.

Kat glowered. "Are you ready?"

"Whoa, *that* look isn't doing your face any favors," Harry said but then dropped his tablet on Helen's writing desk and stood—saluting his mother. "Yes, Sarge, I'm ready to leave for the Christmas Eve pageant at your command."

Kat leaned into him, slipping her arms around his waist. "Stop. You make me miss your brother." Kat glanced at the photo of Nathan in his dress uniform on Helen's bookcase and sighed. "Are you sure we're set up to Skype with him tomorrow?"

"Skype?" Helen asked.

"Video chat, Gran," Harry answered before responding to his mother. "Stop worrying about the Golden Boy for one night. He texted me yesterday from a raging party. Didn't exactly sound like letters from a lonely soldier."

"Nathan can text from Afghanistan?" Helen asked.

"People text from everywhere," Harry said. He turned to Kat with a serious look. "How about this? If it helps, set an extra place tomorrow. I'll eat double, burp the alphabet, and then refuse to help clean up. It'll be like Nathan never left."

Katherine swatted him and laughed. He broke from her to lean in and kiss Helen on the forehead. As he did, Helen grabbed him close with one hand. Reaching beneath her chair pillow, she pulled out two plane tickets and pressed them into his shirt pocket.

"What's this?" he asked, snatching them out and opening the ticket jacket. "Wait? Are you serious? Is this for real?"

"What's she done now?" Kat asked.

Helen nodded, smiling at his joy. "I've saved one gift for the morning, but I couldn't wait to give you those."

Kat read over Harry's shoulder. "Plane tickets? Where?"

"Israel. Two tickets to Israel. I can't believe you did this! When do we leave? Tell me tomorrow night. I'm so ready!" Harry stared as if they might disappear.

"They're open-ended, but I was hoping you could make time during January break. It'll be wonderful to get out of the cold and I'm itching for an adventure."

"Mom, can I? Don't say no! This is amazing!" He looked at his mother, pleading.

Kat threw up her hands. "She spoils you, but yes. You two have been talking about a Mid-East trip since you were ten."

"You're the best, Gran. Absolutely, the best!"

"It's settled then," Helen replied. "Tomorrow afternoon, we'll chart our course. On Monday, I'll call the travel agent."

"We don't have to wait until Monday, Gran. We can arrange everything ourselves over the Internet."

"Surely not on Christmas Day?" she asked.

"You need to catch up with technology, Gran. I'm a technological wizard. I'll show you all my magic tomorrow. Israel! We're going to Israel!" Harry shouted as he jumped and touched the ceiling. "I have a special gift for you, too, Gran, but I was saving it for the morning. Maybe I can arrange to get it to you early."

"No, no. I'm old. I know how to wait for my presents," she said, laughing.

He dashed out the door calling, "Later on, Gran, I'll reenact the Christmas pageant for you. If you won't come to Jesus, I'll bring Jesus here to you!"

Kat put her hands on her hips. "You spoil Harry, but you don't do anything without an agenda. What's your game, Mom?"

"No game. Can't an old woman indulge her grandson?" Helen felt Kat's stare burn into her conscience. "Fine. *And* I think it would help to expand his worldview by experiencing other perspectives and cultures. I'm still hoping he'll reconsider his life path."

"There it is." Kat gave her that *gotcha* look.

Helen shook her index finger. "Harry's mind is wasted at that backwater Christian college. He should be at Brown studying something serious. Why you encourage him in this nonsense about the clergy is beyond me."

"Mom."

"He's gifted, Kat! It pains me no end to see his mind atrophied by religion."

"Harry is where God wants him to be."

"Harry is where you've brainwashed him into being."

"Honestly, I'm not doing this now. It's Christmas Eve."

"And you're abandoning me." Helen stared into her daughter's emerald green eyes, the same eyes she saw in her own mirror every morning. She touched her hand to Kat's thick, auburn hair—this from her father who had been gone two Christmases now. "Who plans an entire evening of church activities on Christmas Eve? Tonight is about family. When you were growing up, we had wonderful Christmases without bringing religion into it. You children turned out beautifully."

"Well, that's stretching it."

"Your sister is fine."

"My sister left her husband and children to go find herself on an ashram in India because she had a spiritual awakening during a Julia Roberts movie."

"Lizzie's creative, bordering on genius like our Harry. You can't expect her to be content in traditional roles. I never was."

"So what does that make me? I'm not intelligent or creative because I'm content being a homeschooling mom?"

"I do wish you were using your education."

"Using my education! I-I-I don't even know what to say to that!" Kat shook her head. "You think Lizzie's way is best? Abandon her kids, break her vows, and shack up with a man who thinks bathing is a capitalist notion?"

"At least she's leading her own life, experiencing the world, and not operating according to archaic mumbo-jumbo. You've fed my grandchildren on fairy tales since birth. Harry, at least, deserves better than to waste his life and mind on an emotional opiate."

15

"Mom—" Kat tried to interrupt, but Helen saw her mission now.

She raised her voice louder than usual, even with Kat. "I won't stop trying to wrest him from your provincial idea of an all-powerful higher being. It's intellectual child abuse to raise him with such a narrow world-view."

Kat's face was as red as her hair and Helen figured tears would follow. Kat was always weepy.

Paul entered just in time. "Ready?" Paul spotted his coat but not before glancing at the two women. "Everything all right?"

"Fine," they snapped.

"All righty, then. Kat, the girls left with Harry. I'll warm up the wagon." He walked across the red and gold Persian carpet to Helen. "Catch you later, Cookie!" He nodded in Kat's direction. "Go easy on the kid. As ornery as you are, she has a soft spot for you." He kissed her cheek, winking as he left pulling on his coat.

"Kat," Helen hoped for mercy, "let's not argue. Sometimes I do envy your faith."

"Don't patronize."

"No, I do. Faith works for someone like you; I see that. But Harry, I truly believe he's more like me."

Kat held up her hand. "If Daddy were here, he'd get you to understand. He eventually accepted the truth."

"Your father had actual guilt that required forgiving. Selling him on a God who paid his debts was just the snake oil an old man needed to alleviate an overburdened conscience."

"Oh, and you've been perfect. You don't need Jesus or forgiveness?" Kat shrugged on her coat, flipping her hair over the collar.

Helen sat tall in her chair, indignant at the notion she might need to beg for pardon, entering heaven like some serial killer or hoodlum.

She grabbed the cane leaning against her chair and pounded the floor with it. "I've led an exemplary life marked by sound decisions and good works. If my life were one of the books I've edited, it would need very little red pen editing to make it worthy of being published in heaven. I dare your God to find enough bad in my life to condemn me. I don't need Jesus, thank you very much. My life is ready to approach the gates of heaven, should it exist, and stand on its own merits."

Paul beeped the horn. "Wow, you win, Mom. Spend tonight here with Scrooge and Gatsby. Do you want me to wake you when we come home?"

"I'll be up."

Kat sighed. "I love you."

As Kat walked out, Helen noticed that Harry's computer tablet was still on her writing table. "Kat! CJ- I mean, Harry forgot—" The sound of the front door closing and then a car door slam indicated that she was, at last, alone.

Helen rose stiffly from her overstuffed chair, grasping the head of her cane and walked to the east window. Narragansett Bay danced below and Helen watched it roll on as it always did, as it always had. She let it quiet her spirit. Lights in the shape of a Christmas tree sparkled from a boat on the water, a glowing star dancing atop it as the vessel bobbed on the waves.

In the darkened glass, she caught her reflection, lit from behind by the yellow lamplight and her small fireplace. Her hair, once a butterscotch brown, was now a lovely white. She was proud it retained its thickness; she wore it in a chin-length bob inspired by Dame Helen Mirren, the actress for whom she was frequently mistaken in younger days.

She picked up Harry's tablet, a flat rectangle, and touched the screen. It sprang to life. On the blue background appeared a quote from the Bible, *For what does it profit a man to gain the whole world and forfeit his soul?* (Mark 8:36)

"Oh." She set it back onto the writing desk and fumed. A Bible verse for a screen-saver. How unimaginative! How would she get through to him? She couldn't save all her grandchildren but just maybe, she could rescue this one.

She sighed. Just not tonight.

"Well, Nellie," she said to the old woman looking back from the window. "Nice work. We're alone on Christmas Eve."

The doorbell chimed and Helen smiled at her reflection. "A visitor? How exciting. See. If you'd gone out looking for this fictional Jesus, you would have missed the real visitor right at your door."

# Chapter 2

Helen pressed her nose against the glass pane of the front door panel. "Who is it?" she called. She switched on the outside light but still saw no one on the stoop. She waited a moment and slipped her hand from the knob of the cane to the neck before opening the door.

There was no one in sight but on the step sat an elaborate gift box with a tag bearing her nickname, "Nellie."

"Hello?" she called out into the crisp night air. "Hello?" Helen pulled the chocolate-brown silk pashmina off its hook and wrapped it around her white men's tailored shirt, thankful she was wearing warm twill slacks as she walked to the end of her sidewalk.

Still no one. Helen looked up and down Sea View Avenue. Deserted. Several homes down the way had clusters of cars spilling out onto the street, but whoever had left the package was a quick mover.

Helen smiled at the cloudless sky and inhaled. She loved this time of year, especially here in Newport. The old-fashioned streetlamps bedecked with greens and ribbons. A Lincoln passed and pulled over two doors down. Greetings rang out from the open entryway. A young couple was ushered into a home brimming with revelers. Suddenly, she felt alone.

Sensing the downshift in her mood, she scolded herself. "Hmph. No reason to feel sorry for yourself, Nellie," she said aloud. "Someone has left you a mystery package and what could be more fun than that on Christmas Eve?"

Inside, she kept her shawl on and placed the package on the stair lift Kat and Paul had installed last week as an early Christmas present. So far, the only one who'd ridden it was Harry. He'd sit and ascend slowly, accompanying her as she maneuvered the stairs one at a time. He'd distract her from her aching joints by prattling on. She'd bristled at the implications of the stair lift but right now, it proved useful.

Back in her study, she set the gift on the white overstuffed chair beside her chair as she made herself a cup of coffee from the single-cup brewer Kat had bought for her father, his final Christmas. Then, in the spirit of the night, she decided the evening called for a special touch, so she "Irished it up" as Charles used to say before he gave up whiskey for Jesus. She added a generous dollop of whipped cream too from the mini-fridge Nathan had given her from his apartment before he deployed.

She loved her little workspace, her private study, where hours of her day passed surrounded by her best friends—words. Charles remodeled this for her when she'd acquired enough editing clients to leave the paper and work full-time from home.

The walls were creamy white with a bay window dominating most of the east wall. Book stacks teetered throughout serving double-duty as stands for extra reading glasses, cookie plates, and mail. The walls that didn't contain books were dappled with diplomas, awards, and photos of Helen with celebrities or politicians she'd interviewed through the years, including two presidents. Other photos captured her laughing, always standing beside Charles, at charity events surrounded by fellow socialites.

The lawyer's desk commanded the rounded window looking out over the Newport cliff walk and onto the Easton section of Narragansett Bay. As she blew on her coffee and took a lick of the whipped cream, she pulled the chain on the amber and brass lawyer's lamp in the center of the desk. She opened the top right hand drawer and removed the false bottom, revealing a stack of printed pages, her latest, and most likely final, project. She ran her fingers over the letters on the cover page—*My Adventurous Life* by Helen Eloise Harper Bancroft. She smiled. She'd had a good life and one of which she was proud.

She'd spent months penning her autobiography, a gift she would entrust to Harry tomorrow. She sipped her coffee and sighed at the buzzy warmth.

The gift.

She'd nearly forgotten.

Turning around, she tilted her head and stared at the package, admiring the understated elegance. Whoever sent it knew precisely what she liked and that made her wonder. Lizzie hadn't sent a gift in years. Much as she defended her younger daughter to Kat, Helen knew that Lizzie was a selfish woman. No, it wouldn't be from Lizzie.

Maybe Nathan? He was thoughtful, but he never would have addressed the package to "Nellie."

A quandary.

She stroked Gatsby's head as she passed the cat sleeping on the Wuthering Heights quilt heaped beside her chair and set her coffee on the stand. She wiggled her backside into the seat and pulled the gift onto her lap.

Helen hesitated before lifting the lid. *What about anthrax? Ridiculous.* She chuckled at her reflexive caution leftover from 9/11. She shook her head at living in times when one suspects a beautiful package of containing a death sentence.

"Open it, Nellie! Merry Christmas, you old fool." The lid slid easily and the contents enchanted her immediately. On top, in a luxurious red and silver lacquered wood case, was an Italian Aurora 85th anniversary, limited edition, red marble fountain pen with several refill cartridges of beautiful blood-red ink.

She'd seen such pens but only in catalogs. It was worth over two thousand dollars. Who would have purchased such a lavish gift? More to the point, who would know how pleased she would be at receiving one?

After admiring her gift, feeling the fit and weight of it in her hand, itching to use it on a manuscript that needed a polish, she noticed that beneath the pen was a note written on eggshell-colored parchment. She slipped on her reading glasses and held the note under her chair lamp.

*My dearest Nellie,*

*I accept your dare.*

*This is your opportunity to prove you can enter heaven on your own merits. Use the pen to edit from your life story anything you've done that requires my forgiveness. If more story remains at the end than what you've edited, I'll admit you were right.*

*There's one catch.*

*You must weigh every edit, the choices you eliminate, and those that remain against the standard in this book. Don't worry that you're not familiar with it. It's a very special version designed to help you with this project.*

*I know you'll be fair.*

*Merry Christmas,*

*God*

Katherine. That wretched girl. Helen's mood darkened. She'd been excited at the thoughtfulness of the pen but now saw it was just part of a sneaky, religious trap. And, how did Kat know about the book? Not from Helen. Kat never snooped, especially not around this room. Lizzie was the snooper. Katherine got nervous watching detectives on TV.

Wait. Harry had caught her working on it when he visited over summer break. He'd hinted about a special gift. This must be his doing.

But the line about the dare? She'd only just made that challenge. Helen glanced about, half expecting to see someone there with her. She listened intently to the rest of the house, but there wasn't a sound, just the pop of logs on the fire.

She sipped the Irish coffee and glanced again at the pen. Putting her cup on the table, she pulled back the gold silk handkerchief inside the box uncovering a rich, brown leather-bound Bible, its title emblazoned in gold along with her engraved name just below.

So predictable.

Still, it was a lovely edition. Literature was literature and she valued all things written. The Bible would make a nice addition to her shelves. She didn't imagine for a minute the words could change her life or her life after death.

Death was death. Others might need the illusion there was more, but Helen was practical. She'd loved Charles every day they were together and missed him every moment since he'd been gone, but she believed the person who was Charles Hadley Bancroft had ceased to exist sometime in the night beside her in the bed they'd shared for fifty-six years, give or take.

She wasn't unfamiliar with the Bible. She'd read large portions as a child in the Presbyterian church her family attended. During the long dry sermons, the Bible was a pleasant distraction. In college, she'd earned an "A" in her course on Biblical literature, but it was more like reading Shakespeare than something mystical or holy.

23

What was that child thinking?

Helen flipped it open, admiring the font and the gold-edged paper, when suddenly the pages turned themselves, settling on one with a passage that shone as if it were backlit.

She started and jerked her hands away. What kind of trick was that?

The note said it was "a special version." It must be like that computer do-hickey on the desk. Helen shut the book and opened it again. Once more, the pages flipped of their own accord, to a page with a passage illuminated as if the ink itself glowed.

Still not touching the Bible, Helen leaned closer to read the highlighted verse:

*Your eyes saw my unformed substance;*

*in your book were written, every one of them,*

*the days that were formed for me,*

*when as yet there was none of them.*

Psalm 139:16

*Well, well. So, God was a writer. I've never considered that.*

Suddenly from across the room came the sound of a baby's cry. Helen swiveled her neck. What was that? Harry's tablet glowed. She grabbed her cane and walked over to see that it was, indeed, the source of the sound of a crying newborn. Across the surface of the screen, floating on a bed of swirling smoke, was the date of her birth, January 5, 1931. No picture displayed but all at once, familiar adult voices rose above the crying.

"Is the baby all right?"

"She's beautiful, Annie."

Father. That was her father's voice. How could that be? She didn't recall any mention of a recording device at her birth, a birth that had taken place in this very room.

"It's a girl?"

"It's a beautiful girl."

"Are you disappointed, Arthur?"

Mother? Was that her mother's voice? It sounded like a voice she knew, but that couldn't be. She'd never heard her mother speak.

"Disappointed? Of course not. We have Arthur Jr. A fourth daughter is just what our little family needs. Shall we name this one after Gran?"

"Helen. Helen Eloise Harper. It's lovely. She's so perfect, so—"

"Annie, what's wrong? Annie? Beatrice, stay with her. I'll fetch Doc Bemis."

Another thin wail from the baby. Then Momma Bea's voice, "Annie! Come back to us, Annie!"

The screen on the tablet went dark and Helen stared at it. Gently, she laid her hand on the face of it as if she could touch her mother somehow, her father, Momma Bea.

How had Harry made this happen? Technology was amazing but where had he found a recording of her birth she didn't know existed? Impossible. She poked the tablet several times but couldn't figure out how to bring it back. Was there more?

She knew the rest of the story from that night. Mother had died and mother's sister, Beatrice, had moved in to care for her and the others. Not long after, father married Momma Bea and more babies followed, born in this same room but not to her mother.

Helen dabbed at the corner of her eye and sniffed. What kind of a trick was this? How did this contraption work and what about the electronic Bible? They must be rigged to work in tandem.

She returned to the chair and examined the binding of the Bible. Looking over the front and back covers, she couldn't locate a button or place for a battery. From all appearances, it was a normal book.

She placed it on the overstuffed chair and decided she'd had enough of the gift tonight. She'd finish her coffee and read her Christmas Eve story. When they got home, she would interrogate her conniving brood until she got answers.

Just as she settled back and opened her novel, the Bible opened on its own and flipped pages until it settled on a different passage, this one nearly at the end of the book. Again, it glowed. Helen ignored it, but finally, curiosity won out and she looked.

*Do not be deceived: God is not mocked, for whatever one sows, that will he also reap* (Galatians 6:7).

"That's exactly my point!" Helen shouted at the book. "I've sown well. I've lived a good life of good decisions. If you exist, you'll reward my good life with entrance to heaven, if that's even real."

Just then, something spooked Gatsby and he skittered across Helen's chair, the breeze of his escape wafting the note back onto Helen's lap.

*Edit my own life story. Prove there's more good that should earn me entrance to heaven than bad that would require forgiveness from God.*

She didn't know how, but perhaps this was her grandson's way of begging her to convince him God didn't exist. *He must be having doubts. Perhaps Harry's afraid to tell his parents, to disappoint them. This could be exactly the way I can reach him, to help him, to prove to him—to all of them—that a person doesn't need Jesus to be good enough for heaven.*

It only takes one good soul to put a monkey-wrench in their entire theology.

*No problem.*

*Why, if they thought I would fear this challenge, they were quite wrong.* This was the opportunity she'd hoped would come her way with Harry. She was confident in the merits of her own life and editing is what she does best.

Helen stared at the red pen.

At once, she snatched it up. After tossing another log onto the fire, she grabbed the Bible and her cane and walked to her desk. She opened the drawer and reached beneath the false bottom, plunking the pages onto the desktop.

As she pulled the cover from the silver nib, she spoke aloud, "You're on, God, or Harry, or whoever you are. My life is one good edit away from perfection. You just watch."

# Chapter 3

Helen turned to chapter one, "Decade of Shattered Innocence." She smiled. Her titles packed a punch. Dramatic, yes, especially for a chapter about life from birth to ten, but then, she was born into dramatic times.

There wouldn't be much requiring forgiveness in her early years but, to be fair, she'd peruse it anyway. She stroked her new pen and settled in for a marathon edit.

Helen wrote an autobiography her family would actually read, a history as engaging as a good novel. She'd divided life into decades and she'd hung the tale, not on trivial, pedestrian events but on select potent memories, ones she could taste and smell when she closed her eyes.

The bristly prickle of Daddy's beard and the scent of his vanilla pipe tobacco when he kissed her goodnight.

Momma Bea's sticky hairspray and the spongy bounce of her short curls in Nellie's chubby hands.

The smooth, rolling feel of cranberries fresh from the bog in the wagon out in the woodshop waiting for Momma Bea to boil them into a tart sauce or bake them into bread.

Gathering around the radio with the whole family after dinner.

Before baby Toby died of polio, there were ten of them. Daddy, Momma Bea, AJ, Mary, Gladys, Maudie, Helen, Dodie, Molls, and Toby. They feasted on a revolving menu of classical music (for Momma Bea), comedy (Gladys and Dodie's favorite), drama (AJ and Mary's pick), or (Daddy and Nellie's favorite) news from around the world. Those evening broadcasts inspired her early love of journalism. Edward R. Murrow's voice was as dear to her as her father's and the staccato notes announcing a CBS news bulletin were the soundtrack behind her ambition to write for newspapers.

One night, in particular, was embedded so firmly in her mind, it was easily her earliest intact memory. She was six. AJ, fifteen, was so excited at dinner he barely ate his meatloaf. Mrs. Adams, his English teacher, had assigned him to write a report to read to the entire school on something called the Hindenburg.

Nellie had no idea what a Hindenburg was except it must be something that flew. AJ was determined to fly. He had confided to her during long afternoons in their tree house that he planned to be a Navy pilot. AJ missed Momma Annie like crazy, more than the rest because he remembered her most. He reasoned the higher he flew, the closer he would be to her.

Nellie wanted that for him. She owed AJ since she was the reason their mother had died, the reason there was no plain "momma" in their family but a Momma Annie and then a Momma Bea. A succession of mothers in alphabetical order. So, when it was time for the broadcast, she made it her job to shush the others and enforce quiet so AJ wouldn't miss a word.

Everyone else sat facing the radio, but Nellie only had eyes for AJ. She knelt at his feet enraptured as he scribbled in his notebook, his eyes wide with excitement as the radio reporter described the approach of the airship.

Zeppelin. That was the only word she remembered from the start of the report. Zeppelin. Zeppelin. She liked the sound of it and rolled it over in her mind as she watched her brother at work. When he was intent on what the announcer said, he squinted and pursed his lips before scribbling more. She was so proud, certain he was meant for greatness.

Then his face changed. It became red and twitchy. Nellie realized the reporter was screaming—his voice a wailing, sorrowful cry through the speaker, and AJ wasn't writing, not writing at all. Tears dripped from his nose and chin as he strained forward in his chair. Momma Bea whisked the little ones from the room, calling Nellie to come along, but Nellie didn't move from her spot at AJ's feet.

The radioman kept yelling about fire, smoke, passengers, and then AJ pulled her into his lap and buried his face in her white cotton shirt. Daddy stared straight ahead from the walnut rocker, his face hard like stone, patting AJ's back. Nellie stroked his shoulder as he held her so tightly his fingers made red marks in her arms. She stared at the notebook and pencil on the floor, his notes smeared by fat wet drops. Nellie tried to absorb his sadness like a sponge, tried to take it all from him so he would never be this sad again.

*Are you watching, God? Do you see? Nothing to forgive here. I loved my brother with a pure, hard love. I even tried to take away his pain. I was a good girl from the start.*

A sip of coffee. Helen continued to read.

Ah, here was something she could strike from the page. On September 20, 1938, seven-year-old Nellie Harper stole a handful of caramels from Browning's Penny Candy store on a dare from Ricky Bolger. Helen drew a red line through the passage describing that event.

*There? Happy? I need forgiveness for stealing. You have me dead to rights. I was a child shoplifter.*

31

Helen stared out the window, remembering her casual, stealthy approach to the counter as old Mr. Browning waited on Penelope Goodwin. Ricky watched from outside to ensure she didn't chicken out. The icy thrill of grabbing the sweets. The sugary flood of pilfered caramel on her tongue as they indulged on the walk home followed by the sour guilt that sucker-punched her as she arrived home.

At dinner, she'd confessed to Daddy. He sent her to bed with no radio time and informed her she'd have to tell Mr. Browning in the morning and find a way to repay him. Unusually alone in the room she shared with five sisters, she cried from shame and vowed never to listen to another stupid boy. She dreaded facing Mr. Browning.

But the next day, a storm like no other roared up the coast. By afternoon, her crime was a distant memory as the family huddled in the basement listening to howling winds, driving rain, and neighbors' houses splintering apart, exploding in the path of the Hurricane of 1938.

On the morning of September 22nd, they emerged to large-scale destruction. Nothing looked right. Nellie followed AJ and Daddy down to the beach. She'd touched her first dead body there. That might be a sin. She glanced at the Bible; she wasn't sure.

She remembered broken boards, sections of houses, parts of boats, and boots and coats everywhere, not realizing at first there were still feet in the boots and bodies in the coats until she squatted for a closer look and there he was. Under a pile of shingles. A dead man.

Sometimes his face still drifted into her dreams. Pasty white and mottled blue. Swollen. Staring. Hair matted flat. A fisherman by the looks of his gear. Harlan Whitford. The name wafted into her memory, but it must be that someone had said the name later on because she didn't recall recognizing the father of Ellie Whitford, a delicate, sickly girl in her class at school. She just remembered reaching out and touching the cold, spongy skin of his bloated hand, then yanking it away when AJ called her name, snatched her up, and carried her back to the house where he ordered her to remain for the rest of the day.

Helen looked back at the manuscript and dragged a red line through that part as she whispered, "Forgive me for touching Ellie Whitford's dad's dead body." She wasn't sure why she felt she needed forgiveness for that, but she did know if it had been her father, she wouldn't have wanted Ellie Whitford poking him out of curiosity.

The rest of the chapter contained select details about family life, school, her father and her siblings, memories she wanted Harry to pass on to the next generation. Helen set her pen down and stretched.

*That's all for that decade, God. Sorry to disappoint but I wasn't much of a sinner from birth to ten.*

She was about to turn to chapter two when Harry's tablet sprang to life.

Helen gasped. On the screen, a little girl with butterscotch braids sat on the front pew of the First Presbyterian Church of Newport—hands clasped, eyes closed, and lips moving in prayer.

"No," whispered Helen. "Not that. Not that day." She shook her head, but she couldn't look away as the scene played. *Where did Harry get this? Impossible to have this footage. Not this.*

Nellie Harper, ten-years-old, her feet swinging inches above the floor, prayed in the darkened church. "Please don't let him die. Please, God. Save AJ. Let him be safe. Don't let the bombers get him. Please, God, not AJ Save him from the Japanese. Bring him home safe from Pearl Harbor."

She watched her younger self rocking until she dozed off still upright, hands clasped. A man in a gray suit and wingtip shoes walked down the aisle.

"Daddy?" He was so young. His hair still dark, standing tall. Helen touched the border of the tablet with her finger. She felt a catch in her diaphragm. "Daddy," she whispered as she watched.

Stooping, he lifted little Nellie into his arms and carried her home. In the next scene, the sun shone through the church window and Nellie burst through the door out of breath, wearing yesterday's overalls, braids frayed. She dashed to the front pew and resumed praying. "God, please. We need to hear from AJ. Please keep AJ alive."

Others stopped by the sanctuary throughout the day to pray or to comfort. Momma Bea, red-eyed, stood in the back of the room with other mothers, some collapsing when news arrived about their own sons, some advising her what to do about Nellie. Several times, Nellie's older sisters enticed her to eat or to come home, but she shook them off and kept praying.

A second nightfall, a darkened church and there was Daddy again, lifting her from where she'd fallen asleep on the hardwood floor. Silently, he carried her through the dark streets, laying her gently on the sofa in their front room. He smoothed a lock of hair from her face, touched his palm to her cheek, and then collapsed into the chair beside her where he too prayed himself to sleep.

People remember December 7, 1941, but the bombs dropped for Helen on the morning of December 9th when she woke up on the scratchy scarlet davenport to the sound of a car in the gravel drive. Now, on Harry's tablet, she saw herself sit up and rub her eyes.

She watched the black government car pull to a stop and held her breath as three men in uniform, one of them carrying a Bible, walked up the front steps. Nellie slipped off the sofa and shook Daddy's arm so he too saw the car. Slowly, like an old man, Daddy stood, then waited with his hand on her shoulder for the sound of knocking before walking to the door.

Nellie remained frozen in place by the chair.

"Mr. Harper, we regret to inform you …"

Daddy sobbed a giant, racking sob and stumbled backward into the room until he landed hard on the wooden bench amidst the galoshes and umbrellas. Momma Bea, still in her housecoat, rushed to him from the kitchen doorway, shouting to her sisters to fetch the doctor. The Navy chaplain leaned over Daddy and patted his arm. "Your son died a hero, sir."

Nellie watched as the doctor and neighbors arrived to help Daddy, to comfort Momma Bea, to bring food and discuss arrangements. She stood for hours beside the wooden bench where Daddy had landed. Everyone moved around her as if she wasn't there and truly, some part of her had ceased to exist.

All at once, she shoved past the mourners, dashed out the door and ran down the streets back to church. There, she hurled rocks at the windows, successfully shattering seven panes of stained glass before the pastor snatched her up and carried her kicking and screaming back home.

Helen slapped her palm down on the tablet and the image went dark.

"Is that my sin, God? Is that what you're holding against me? Do I need forgiveness that on the day my brother died, I vowed to never talk to you again? Do I need forgiveness for hating you for not protecting A.J? Hating you that Daddy's heart was never the same? All AJ wanted was to fly to be close to Momma Annie! But, you couldn't give him that! You had to take his life too and for nothing. It was all for nothing!"

Helen's hand shook as she hovered the nib of her pen over the manuscript. It had to be a sin to stop praying and even without that flipping Bible she knew it was wrong to hate God if He existed. If she were going to be fair, she would have to write this scene and then edit this part out. She waited, though until the paper dried from where her tears fell.

"But if I need forgiveness for this, God, you need forgiveness for it, too." Her words were an angry whisper, but then the Bible turned its own pages again.

*When I was a child, I spoke like a child, I thought like a child, I reasoned like a child. When I became a man, I gave up childish ways. For now we see in a mirror dimly, but then face to face. Now I know in part; then I shall know fully, even as I have been fully known* (1 Corinthians 13:11-12.)

Helen shrugged. "I don't get it. Is that supposed to mean something? If it's a message, I don't understand it. Of course, I thought like a child, I was a child. As were AJ and most of the boys who died that day. It was all pointless. Easier for me to believe you don't exist than to accept that you stepped aside and watched my brother die in vain."

Helen realized she'd spoken aloud and she shook her head at her reflection in the windowpane. "Don't lose it now, old girl. Remember, this isn't about God, it's about Harry. Keep at it. Don't be silly. Who do you think you're talking to? No one's listening. On to the next chapter."

# Chapter Four

"A Decade on the Frontlines." That's how she remembered those next ten years. Her world was a battleground. World War. War in Europe. War in the Pacific. War at home. The war a child wages forging her way through adolescence. Sins wouldn't be hard to find in this chapter, but they were minor transgressions. *The follies of youth. So what?* Defiant, she readied her pen.

First, there were the rocks she threw at Donnie Yeager. What did she know? She was eleven. For weeks, she joined the other schoolchildren torturing Donnie for being German. He wasn't, of course, he was as American as they were, but that was a technicality.

Donnie's dad was the butcher. He'd come to America alone in his late teens. Donnie's mother's family arrived when she was a child. Mrs. Yeager worked as a seamstress. Before the war, her dresses were in demand but everything changed. The Yeagers were German and all Germans were suspect. That's what the older boys told them.

So, she threw rocks at Donnie and called him ugly names she learned from the boys and only half understood. When Momma

Bea made her address a Christmas card to him along with the ones for the rest of her classmates, she tore it up and buried it by the fence before school. Dodie and Molls saw her do it.

"Why you always so mean to that boy, Nellie?" Dodie asked swiping her plump fist across her runny nose.

"Don't you know? Germans killed AJ."

"Nuh-uh," said Molls pushing her glasses up on her nose. "Mary said Japanese bombers killed AJ."

"It's the same, baby girl. Germans, Japanese. All enemies. Don't you know nuthin'?"

"You used to like Donnie, back in fourth grade, Nellie," Dodie said.

"Lots of things were different in fourth grade."

One month later, Mary eloped with Donnie's older brother, Peter. That made Nellie's life even worse. She had to take drastic measures to prove herself a loyal American now. Daddy and Momma Bea told her she was being overly sensitive. Everyone in town was not talking about them and no one suspected they were spies just because Mary ran off with a Yeager. She couldn't make them understand so it fell to Nellie to defend the family reputation.

That's how she found herself, late one Saturday night, helping Ricky Bolger and Whitey Long set fire to the Yeagers' barn. When they were planning it in Ricky's backyard after school, it seemed like a perfectly rational idea. This was her part in the war effort like rolling bandages and going without meat.

But looking at the Yeagers' little farmhouse with the roof that needed repair and the blackout curtains in the windows, Nellie started to lose her nerve. She stopped at the edge of the property.

Whitey nudged her. "Hey, you ain't chickening out, are you, Harper?"

Ricky defended her. "She's no Kraut-lover, are you, Nellie? I told you, Whitey, she won't back down."

"Her sister's a Kraut-lover. She's probably comforting the enemy right now." Whitey winked and laughed, grunting in the moonlight in a way that made Nellie want to get the whole thing over with quickly. She snatched the box of matches out of Whitey's hand.

"I'll show you who's American. Wait out here." She slipped into the barn and struck a match. Holding it up, she scanned the room until she spotted a lantern on the west wall. It was weirdly quiet, empty of animals. Nellie was willing to burn a building, but her conscience wouldn't let her hurt innocent beasts. She'd snuck in an hour before and led them all into the back pasture before meeting the boys. It made it easier to spill lamp oil onto a hay bale before setting the hay alight.

The blaze exploded faster than she'd imagined it would. For several minutes, she stood mesmerized as the flames scrambled up the barn walls and around through the dry hay. She heard someone yell and turned to escape the way she came in, only now the barn was full of smoke and the ring of fire had spread fast so that she was confused and couldn't see the door. She spun around, trying to think clearly.

Sputtering and coughing, her eyes tearing, she stumbled back the way she thought she'd come only to feel a hard, unmoving wall against her palms. Her fingers filled with splinters as she pounded on the wood, running her hands across beams looking for a door. Her throat was scratchy, thick and sore. Her eyes—gritty and dry. Her breaths came fast and shallow. She spun around again but everything looked the same and her cheeks felt as though she'd held them up against Momma Bea's flat iron. She tried to call out, but her voice was a raspy bark. What had she done?

Nellie never knew if it had been Ricky or Whitey who came for her but suddenly there were hands on the back of her shirt propelling her through a smaller doorway out of the inferno and into the cool night.

She collapsed onto the snow, gulping the frosty air, coughing, and spitting out black sooty globs. She heard feet crunching through the woods and knew those stupid boys had left her alone to save their own hides. At least, one of them had dragged her to safety. From the direction of the farmhouse came voices and the sound of trucks as neighbors arrived to help. An explosive pop and the crack of beams caving hastened her recovery. She staggered to her feet and slipped into the woods, running all the way home without looking back.

Helen looked over at the Bible and held up her hand. "Don't even bother opening. I'm clear on the fact that setting people's barns on fire classifies as a sin." She took her red pen to the page but glanced up as the tablet glowed.

There they were on the screen: Nellie, Whitey, and Ricky, running through the back woods towards the Yeagers, the same scene she'd just read in her book but, on the tablet, several hundred feet behind them strode a taller figure. The camera zoomed in and she recognized her father in his winter walking coat and boots.

What was Daddy doing there? She didn't remember that.

As the three arsonists stood arguing outside the barn, Daddy huddled behind a tree, listening and slapping his arms for warmth. She watched herself run into the barn. Daddy circled round to the other side out of sight of the boys. Once he reached the opposite wall, Daddy slid into the barn and witnessed silently as she set the blaze.

From where he stood, she saw herself stare at the fire. "Move, you fool! Move! Why are you just staring?" she urged the girl on screen. Daddy must of been thinking the same thing because he started toward her but tripped over the connecting arm of a cranberry wagon and fell hard, hitting his head on the blade of a plow. He lay there motionless as the barn filled with smoke and Nellie turned around looking to escape.

Helen spoke to the figure on the screen as if she were there. "Daddy! Get up! What's wrong? Get out!" How could this be?

Daddy's lips moved as he touched a hand to his bleeding head. The camera zoomed in close enough she could hear him. "Jesus, get her out of here. Please. She doesn't know what she's done. Get her to safety, Lord." He struggled, rising to his hands and knees like a prizefighter, shaking his head as though he was dizzy, confused. "Nellie. Nellie," he whispered before collapsing onto the hard-packed floor, smoke swirling thicker around him.

That's when Helen saw a light shining on the other side of the barn. Inside the light was a figure. A man who glowed as if he was on fire too only he wasn't in pain or struggling. He walked through the flames like a man walking through his own sunny meadow. In only a moment, he reached the frightened girl banging blindly against a wall with no door.

His brilliant white hands grasped her shirt and propelled her through the flames as if she was a barn cat, depositing her outside before disappearing back into the burning structure. She watched as the same man made his way to her father and lifted him up as if a child, leaving him unconscious by the barn door closest to the farmhouse.

"Officer, over here! It's Art Harper!" A group of neighbors pulled her father away from the blaze. The glowing man disappeared or maybe the glow had been a trick of the flames and he had only blended into the crowd. The fire involved the entire structure now and there was nothing more anyone could do but stand aside while it burned.

Daddy regained consciousness, propped up against the well housing. Officer John squatted beside him yelling, "What do you know about this, Art? You trying to get back at Hermann for Peter and Mary? I wouldn't have figured you for a caper like this, but you'd better start talking."

Helen's hands trembled. She set the pen down and took a sip of coffee, using both hands to lift the cup.

Her father licked his lips and tried to speak, nodding. "I-I—"

Donnie pointed, shouting. "He's confessing! You hear that everybody? Mr. Harper burned our barn!"

Daddy waved his hand but seemed too overcome to speak.

The officer said, "Art, I never thought I'd say this to you, but I'm going to have to take you in."

"No!" Mr. Yeager, his hair wild from sleep, wearing only boots, an unbuttoned black coat and long johns now covered with soot, pushed through the crowd. "Arthur Harper is a good man. We've been neighbors for years. He would never do this, never. I won't let you arrest him."

The officer pushed his cap back. "Hermann, everyone's doing crazy things these days."

Mr. Yeager interrupted. "No. Arthur is not like everyone. He is a Christian man. Can't you see? He's injured. In the morning, he'll explain." Mr. Yeager turned to his wife, her hair in a cap, plump calves spilling from her nightgown into her galoshes. "Make up the parlor bed for him, Mama. We'll dress his wound and let him rest."

Turning to the crowd, Mr. Yeager continued with tears in his eyes, "You are all such fine, wonderful neighbors. I can never thank you for coming to help, but I will try. I am sure this was just a terrible accident. There's no more to do tonight. Go home, my friends."

He propped Daddy's arm over his shoulder and Donnie grabbed Daddy's other shoulder. Together, they helped him into their home as the others returned to theirs.

Helen leaned back in her chair as the screen went black. *How is this happening? How does the person who sent this package know more about my story than I do?*

She grabbed her cane and cup. She needed more coffee. As she waited for the single cup to brew, she remembered how Daddy helped Mr. Yeager rebuild. A snatch of conversation overheard after bedtime, an argument between Momma Bea and Daddy suddenly made sense.

"But why are you paying for the materials? I don't understand why you think you need to do this," Momma Bea.

There was a pause before Daddy answered. "They're our neighbors. Others have treated them badly with no reason."

"Well," answered Momma Bea, "I hope people are kind to our other friends. We're doing well, but we can't afford to rebuild everyone's barn."

None of it made sense to her. Why had Daddy never told her he knew what she'd done? Who did know and who was the glowing man?

Helen splashed another dash of whiskey into her cup but skipped the whip cream this time. Suddenly she wished she had learned how to text with her new phone. She could contact Harry quietly during the church service. Certainly, he would explain how he'd managed all of this.

She glanced at the clock. Hours, still, before anyone would be home. She might as well continue this strange edit. The reporter in her itched to see this thing through—to follow the story wherever it led.

She returned to the desk.

Helen read several pages of good deeds. Apparently inspired by her stint as an arsonist, Nellie had immersed herself in good works. She tutored younger children. She helped Momma Bea with her sisters and the house. She rolled bandages for the war effort and wrote letters to injured soldiers. She studied and did well in school. "You've got nothing on me here, God."

Oops, spoke too soon. Helen skimmed the paragraphs describing how she'd cheated on three exams when she was fourteen, but that was when the household had come down with the flu, everyone except Molls and her. She'd spent six weeks up late caring for sick parents and siblings and hadn't had time to study. Tommy Atkins' grades were almost as good as hers so, she'd peeked at his tests.

*Who could blame me? Fine,* she red-penned it, *but, seriously, with Hitler creating worldwide havoc, is God really going to hold up my entrance to heaven on a schoolgirl cheat?*

Helen smiled as she read the last section. One month later, Newport buzzed with excitement when Americans sank a German U-boat off Point Judith and not long after that, Germany surrendered. In August, the bombs dropped on Hiroshima and Nagasaki and the war ended.

There were fireworks that night. Fireworks, ice cream at dinner, and dancing in the streets. Even Momma Bea and Daddy, who were not given over to public affection, waltzed in the front yard as the neighborhood celebrated the end of a war that had taken too many of their men too soon. The unfettered joy was a buoyant memory.

Her emotions sank in the wave of the years following. Nellie wasn't prepared for the boys to come home. She thought she'd moved past losing AJ but as men returned from war, so did the pain of her loss. That's why, as she eventually came to understand, she'd convinced herself that she loved Montgomery Salinger.

# Chapter Five

The Salingers had old money. Momma Bea explained this the night of the Christmas Cotillion the Salingers hosted when Monty returned from the Veteran's Hospital in 1947. As she tamed Nellie's hair with the round brush, pins, and hairspray, Momma Bea tutored her on party etiquette.

Daddy had made money during the war—boatloads—designing a widget instrumental in the automatic detonation of bombs. He'd started with family assets but really, Momma Bea explained, he was a self-made man. The Salingers, on the other hand, had always had money, apparently a preferable condition. In her estimation, they were as close to royalty as America had since we'd rebelled against "them Brits".

Old money. To Nellie, the phrase evoked the scent of mothballs, liniment, and musty coats. Still, it animated Momma Bea's face, both with excitement that Nellie was invited, and determination her stepdaughter wouldn't make a single misstep in manners. Not to mention that tonight, Momma Bea emphasized, Nellie might meet a man who'd be fool enough to marry her.

Marriage became epidemic after the war. Mary and Peter settled in upstate New York and would visit in the spring, bringing with them one-year-old Harry and newborn, Bess. Gladys and Maudie had both found GIs with military careers. Gladys was posted in Sicily and Maudie on a base in the Southern California desert, both of them with spring babies due.

At sixteen, Nellie was entirely uninterested in marriage. She had her mind set on a newspaper career. Since her sisters were already sprouting grandchildren, Daddy agreed to send her to Brown after high school. This was the only future that occupied her thoughts.

Still, it was exciting to swirl about in a velvet party dress the color of emeralds and her eyes. Dodie and Molls sighed as she danced around the living room and wished they were old enough to go. The evening was even more thrilling since Daddy was on a trip to DC so he'd arranged a car and driver to deliver her to the soiree and pick her up precisely at midnight.

Newport was aglow with lamplight and greens. The ships in the harbor twinkled with Christmas candles. Couples walked arm in arm, women on the arms of uniformed men. Clusters of people strolling the streets or spilling out of homes and taverns made it seem the whole town was celebrating this year. The night was warm for December and Nellie let her wrap droop low on her back as she stepped from the car, so everyone could see the magnificent detailing of her gown.

An older crowd gathered at the Salingers, but they included Nellie out of deference to AJ's memory. Monty was two years younger than AJ, but they'd been best friends. Daddy used to call them "the twins" because Monty ate at the Harper household more often than he ate at his own. He'd written Daddy long letters from the war, starting shortly after AJ died and right up until the Japanese took him captive.

Monty's father visited shortly after the war ended. Nellie stood on the top stair catching bits of conversation between the men. Monty had been detained on a "hell ship" for months until he reached a POW camp in Japan. There, he'd seen other prisoners die under torture and his father said Monty "snapped." They lowered their voices, but Nellie slipped down the staircase and learned that was why Monty didn't return home right away with the others. He was receiving treatment at a "top-notch facility." His father had every hope that Monty would "return to us whole by Christmas."

It had actually taken two Christmases for the doctors to make Monty whole enough to come home, but now he was here. Nellie waved to several familiar faces as she walked the marble steps to the Salinger mansion doors.

As she crossed the threshold, Nellie could barely take in the magnificence that awaited in the foyer. Candle-laden Christmas trees guarded either side of a sweeping marble staircase leading to the private quarters. The banister was adorned with greens dotted with red velvet bows. Stacks of Christmas gift boxes, red poinsettias, and over-sized pine cones tipped with gold glaze decorated every corner that wasn't occupied by candles and trays of shrimp, cheese, and pastries. Music and chatter drew her to the ballroom on her left, as one waiter took her wrap and another offered her a glass of champagne, which she declined.

That's where she was standing when she spied Monty for the first time since he'd left for boot camp a lifetime ago. From the parquet edge of the dance floor, already filled with couples swirling in time to the eight-piece orchestra, Nellie locked eyes across the room with a taller, broader, more dashingly handsome version of the gangly boy who used to sit beside her at dinner before they all crashed into the war.

It took him only six long strides to reach her and just a moment more for her to fall into the deep blue pools of his long-lashed eyes. Did he even ask her to dance? Did she reply? She never could recall but with one electric touch of his left palm to her right, they were twirling as one to The Blue Skirt Waltz. As they danced, her mind was a whirlwind of questions. Had his hair always been the color of corn silk? Had his arms always been this strong? Had he always smelled of the heady scent of bay rum?

"I can't believe this beautiful woman in my arms is you, Nellie Harper," he shouted over the music as he guided her expertly around the floor.

"I'm sixteen now," she stupidly replied.

"Remember what your brother and I used to call you?" he said with a grin.

"If you start calling me 'Smelly Nellie,' I'll walk right off this dance floor and leave you standing alone, Monty Salinger."

His reply was to pull her sharply toward him and strengthen his grip on her right hand. When the song ended, he held her in the same embrace for just a moment longer than was proper. As everyone politely applauded the musicians, he stood behind her pressing his lips against her ear and whispered, "I miss him something awful tonight, don't you, Nellie-girl?"

She inhaled sharply and nodded.

He went on, "It should have been him that made it through, not me. He was the one with a future. I was born MIA. I shouldn't be here, Nellie-girl. Dance with me, again, will you? Dance with me all night, Nellie."

After that, the evening was perfection. Monty never left her side and by the end of the cotillion, she forgot she'd ever dreamed any other dream than this new one, to be in love forever with Monty Salinger. Even when his klutzy friend, smelling of menthol and mint like her dad and droning on about his medical studies at Brown, spilled his champagne on the corner of her dress, they just laughed.

"Stick with me, Nellie Harper. I'll buy you a hundred ball gowns to replace the one my oafish friend, Mr. Bancroft, has soiled." Monty knelt and dabbed at the hem of her skirt with his handkerchief.

"I'm so sorry, Miss Harper. I usually hold my liquor better, but one glance at you and my hand was strangely unsteady," said the young man with the auburn hair and brown eyes.

"Don't be silly, Charles," she laughed. "Nothing could ruin this night for me. Nothing at all." She and Monty twirled off again laughing, leaving Charles staring after them from the bar.

That night was followed by months of cotillions, lunches on the East lawn, long walks on the beach, and concerts in the park. It was a blur of velvet dresses, black ties and tails, and long-stemmed crystal. Only two other nights with Monty distinguished themselves in her memory—worthy of a few precious lines in her life story.

A little over one year from that first Christmas cotillion, Nellie turned seventeen on a snowy January night. She had a lovely dinner with her family followed by cake and dancing with friends in town. Monty was unusually attentive because she'd agreed at Thanksgiving she would let him make love to her on the night of her birthday celebration.

They were going to be married after all. Everyone understood that by their first spring together but Monty was learning his father's business and Nellie still had to complete high school before they could even think of planning a wedding. She certainly couldn't expect a man who'd been to war to wait that long and it was 1949 after all. The world was changing and Nellie was ready to change with it.

They drove back to the Salinger estate after the festivities and Monty pulled into the heated garage. There, they retired to his father's brand new Royal Maroon Chrysler New Yorker. For years,

Nellie couldn't see Tartan plaid fabric or smell the musk of red leather without flashing back to the night she gave herself to him, believing they would share one love forever.

When it was over, she expected him to be deliriously happy but instead, he cried in her arms, mumbling over and over, "I'm sorry, AJ. I'm so sorry." It would be the only time they ever made love.

Two months later, she sat beside Charles at a wine-infused birthday celebration in Monty's honor in the elaborate Salinger formal dining room. As Monty regaled the gathering of family and friends with fantastical tales of his adventures with AJ in Hawaii before the war broke out, Nellie and Charles shared quiet editorial remarks having heard these tales more times than they could tell.

"How big do you think the waves will be this time?" she asked Charles.

"With this crowd? Twenty-feet at least." Charles had perfected a skill of the privileged, being able to mutter snide comments while managing to appear enrapt with the speaker.

"And how near to death will AJ be before Sir Monty comes to his rescue?" she asked.

"It's his birthday so I imagine he'll have drowned and it will be left to our hero to resurrect him," Charles muttered as she giggled behind her napkin.

When the doorbell rang, it wasn't a concern of anyone's except the butler's until a woman's voice cried out from the foyer followed by murmuring male voices.

"Monty! Monty Salinger! Bring him here. He'll tell you who I am, I say!" screamed the woman.

The men spoke again and Nellie couldn't hear them, but one glance at Monty's face and she felt an instant catch in her chest, a fear she couldn't name but was about to face in the same marble hallway she'd entered that first Christmas.

"Everyone, please carry on. I'll see to this," Monty said as he rose and walked out of the room. He smiled, but his face was the color of the boiled potatoes.

"That's him! That's Monty!" The woman screamed again.

Nellie glanced at Charles. They rose and joined Monty in the foyer.

There stood a young woman barely clothed in a worn cotton dress covered with tiny flowers, knit hat, bare legs, unlaced boots, and a threadbare coat that wouldn't close around her large belly. Her hair was brown and stringy and her eyes, one of which was blackened, were sunken into her pale face. Nellie had seen women like her in the poorer houses near the wharf. Most of them were working girls who greeted the boats when they docked. This one now stood between two police officers in the Salinger foyer and pointed a confident finger at Monty.

"That's my Monty. Tell them, love. Tell them how that justice-of-the-peace married us over in Portsmouth on Pearl Harbor day. Tell them," she whined.

One officer kept hold of the woman's arm as he spoke. "This woman's landlord said she owes him back rent. When he came to collect it, she assaulted him but she's insisting she's your wife, Mr. Salinger, and she does have this."

The officer held out a document, but Monty didn't reach for it. He just stared at the young woman who stared back at him, one hand rubbing her belly. Nellie looked from Monty to the woman and felt the floor shift beneath her. Charles stepped forward and took the document from the officer. He read it quietly, then walked up to Monty and landed a solid right hook onto Monty's perfect face.

Monty caught himself against the wall and held his cheek but didn't retaliate. He never once looked at Nellie. Her limbs quivered and dinner soured in her belly. Charles walked to her and placed one arm around her shoulder and one hand on her arm, dropping the marriage license onto the floor. "Niles, get Miss Harper's wrap, won't you? Come along, Nell. I'll take you home."

She'd ended that chapter there.

Helen set her pen down and leaned back, grabbed her coffee, and glanced over at the tablet. Nothing. No mysterious scene to answer the question of betrayal.

She stared out over the ocean thinking about nothing for several long minutes except the strains of "The Blue Skirt Waltz" played over in her mind.

# Chapter Six

Deciding she needed a new mental soundtrack as she read the next decade, "P.S. I Love You," Helen slid the *Greatest Hits of 1953* into her CD player. Harry gave it to her for Christmas when he was ten. The song by the Hilltoppers that inspired her chapter title was the one she and Charles chose for their wedding dance in 1954 and then, again, for their fiftieth anniversary. She listened to it play through before she slipped the pen back into her hand and resumed editing.

The years between twenty-one and thirty comprised one of the two best decades of her life. The Christmas after her relationship ended with Monty, she traveled with her father to New York City on business. Charles surprised her there with a romantic dinner and tickets for the new Broadway smash, *South Pacific*. He proposed that night in the lobby of the Carlyle Hotel with Gershwin music from the Carlyle Cafe in the background and him smelling of Mennen Skin Bracer and Jameson's.

They agreed to wait until she'd graduated from Brown and he'd completed his residency. Father approved their plans, freeing Nellie, at last, to set aside everyone's concerns about her romantic future and pursue her studies.

The years at Brown were a blurry montage of library, coffee, and assignments. Summers she interned at the town paper and then the *Providence Journal*, first gopher and then grunt—the writer who covered whatever no one else would cover. She and Charles barely saw one another but when they did, it was an easy fit.

Only once did they encounter Monty and Vivian. It was September 1953 at the reception for JFK and Jackie at Hammersmith Farm. A glorious day, both because Charles was off from the hospital and because Nellie had the opportunity for a real story. She scribbled notes throughout the gala. She planned to pitch her first serious feature about the political potential of Robert Kennedy. While most guests were eyeing the fashions and celebrities, Nellie listened in on side conversations noting casual alliances among the powerful friends of the Kennedy clan.

Charles insisted she join him for at least one dance. He was confident and accomplished on the dance floor. They were the pair to watch. When they stopped to catch their breath, they bumped into Monty and Vivian quietly arguing by the punch bowl.

"Not here, Montgomery. Please. It's too early in the day," Vivian pleaded.

Monty drew a silver flask from his jacket pocket and tipped it over his glass. "Don't be such a nervous ... Nellie and Charles!" As Monty acknowledged them, he screwed the lid back onto his flask with one hand and slipped it into his pocket like the most practiced slight-of-hand artist. "I'd heard rumors you two were together and here you are in the flesh. Mm-mm, Nellie Harper, look at you."

Vivian stared at the grass as Nellie glared at Monty. "Montgomery. Vivian."

Charles touched her elbow. "Good to see you both. Are you enjoying the reception?"

"It's lovely. Like a fairy tale." Vivian looked up and smiled shyly.

She shriveled though as Monty rolled his eyes. "My wife is easily impressed. This is nothing. All show. I could tell you stories about the groom that would seem less like fairy tales and more like those trashy romances they sell at the five-and-dime if you know what I mean." Monty winked.

"I'm sure I don't," Charles responded. "What are you doing these days, Monty? I heard you're no longer working for your father."

Nellie was impressed at the transformation in Vivian since that day in the foyer. Her green, violet, and white garden party dress with the flat, rounded collar perfectly accented by her green heels and clutch were impeccable. Her hair was bobbed in a style that mimicked the bride. Her eyes though had the same sunken look as the day Nellie walked out of Monty's life.

"My interests lie outside the scope of my father's work. I'm a visionary, Charles. My father doesn't appreciate that but I'm on the verge of a deal with a very important man who does appreciate me," Monty said as Vivian straightened the front of her skirt and looked from Charles' face to her husband's.

"And what keeps you busy, Vivian?" Nellie asked.

Vivian opened her mouth, but Monty answered for her. "Vivian has all she can handle keeping our home up to standards and raising Monty Jr, don't you, dear?"

The rest of the conversation was white noise as Nellie focused on the panicked sadness in Vivian's eyes.

Helen had wrestled with how to capture that look of sadness in words in her autobiography. She knew her family would want to read choice details about the famous Kennedy wedding, but she'd been too busy working her connections to be impressed with American royalty so most of the event was hazy, like seeing one's reflection in a steamy mirror.

She stared again at the sea and thought how close she had come to being Vivian. Her life's path could have had a completely different trajectory. That wedding was a pivotal point in her career and Helen congratulated herself again for making smart choices.

She was about to turn the page when the Bible flew open as if it was hit by a twister. It stopped at a glowing passage in the book of James. *Consider what a great forest is set on fire by a small spark. The tongue also is a fire, a world of evil among the parts of the body. It corrupts the whole body, sets the whole course of one's life on fire, and is itself set on fire by hell* (James 3:5b-6).

Helen felt her face heat up. She huffed and spoke aloud in case God was actually listening. "I hope you're referring to Monty. I certainly didn't stand there and boast!"

A tittering wave of women's laughter splashed from Harry's tablet and Helen pulled it closer to watch another scene from the wedding, one she hadn't included in her autobiography. She was standing with a group of women, Newport socialites, prodding them gently for Kennedy gossip.

One of them, sporting a string of pearls and fire red lipstick, pointed at Monty and leaned in. "Tell me about that one. He must be related to the groom, yes?"

A redhead with cat glasses rolled her eyes. "Don't be silly. That's Montgomery Salinger. Nellie was speaking with him earlier, weren't you, Nel? Give us the dish."

"Well," Nellie debated only a moment before speaking. "He's all boast and no backup, that one. And," she paused for dramatic effect, "you know his wife was a wharf woman, don't you?"

The circle gasped and made similar exclamations. "No." "A wharf woman?" "Are you sure?" "Like the ones who greet the sailors?" "For cash?"

Nellie nodded and winked, "Monty's obviously put considerable money into cleaning her up, but if you stand close I promise you there's no mistaking the odor of low tide."

"Oh, Nellie, you're awful!" The cat glasses woman exclaimed. The others nattered on, but Nellie's work was done. When she turned, she nearly fell over Vivian, who stood with arms limply at her side, eyes wide and glassy with tears. They stared at one another for a long moment until Vivian, tears dripping from her nose, put her hands to her cheeks and looked at the ground, clearly in agony.

Helen watched her younger self look with disgust at the poor girl and walk off to find Charles. The screen went dark.

Helen talked to the Bible as if it might talk back. "What? I'm supposed to feel badly about a snide remark? If you're going to call that sin, this is going to be a long, red decade because words were my best weapons. I used words to make my mark, to create my place in that society, to forge my career, but they were just words. I never hurt anyone."

The screen came to life again. Still the reception.

Vivian blowing her nose. Monty strode over and grabbed her upper arm, pressing his mouth to her ear, "What did you say to Nellie, huh? What did you talk about?"

"Nothing. Honest. I was coming to join the others as she walked away," Vivian stuttered.

Monty's face twisted. "You stay right beside me. You're not like these women. They're ladies and Nellie is the best of them. You're nothing like them and you never will be, understand? You're only here because of me. Don't forget it. You'll never belong here. You're just lucky I saved you and didn't let you wash down the gutter with the rest of the street trash."

Vivian nodded in response. Another couple greeted Monty. The men discussed a business deal while the wife snubbed Vivian. Vivian, twisting a lace handkerchief, glanced about like a panicked colt. She stopped a passing waiter carrying long-stemmed glasses of champagne. Her expression changed. Harder, somehow, resolute. She grabbed a glass, placed a hand on the waiter to hold him there, downed the contents in one uninterrupted draft, replaced her empty on the tray and took another.

The screen went gray.

"Well, I will not sit here and take responsibility for that woman's drinking problem, if that's what you're saying. I certainly didn't pour champagne down her throat. I'll admit my words were cruel—even a sin, fine, there must be some Bible verse about unkindness—but I didn't cause all of that with just words."

The screen flickered.

Rain battered a small group of mourners huddled beneath black umbrellas fighting to hold their shape in the biting wind. Nellie and Charles stood arm-in-arm near the back of the crowd. As the minister said, "Amen," the cluster shifted, providing her a clear view of a rose-covered coffin.

Rhoda Mars.

Helen gasped. The tablet sparked memories she would rather keep at bay. "I didn't cause that woman's death. Everyone agreed I couldn't be held responsible," she whispered aloud.

Her editor, Jim Daniels, stood on the other side of Charles. He leaned toward her. "Heck of a thing, Nel. No one saw this coming," he said. Then turning to Charles, "Don't let her beat herself up. I need her behind her desk on Monday."

Nellie hesitated as Charles turned to leave. Beside the simple coffin stood two tow-headed children. A boy, seven and a girl, five.

The boy held his sister's hand. "Just put the flower on Mummy's box, Meribel. To show we love her."

"Why is Mummy in the box, Georgie?" asked the child as she followed instructions.

"She was very tired. Too tired to wake up. Daddy says now she'll sleep forever."

The blonde tyke whispered at the coffin, "Night-night, Mummy."

Nellie looked away only to catch Rhoda's husband's gaze. She expected hatred or condemnation. They contained only sadness.

She softened momentarily, but then fought against it, using Jim Daniels' words to reinforce her mental flak jacket. She'd done nothing wrong. She'd written the truth. That was the job. People make choices.

Rhoda Mars had covered up for her boss, an insignificant politician committing voter fraud and, after Nellie's article came out, investigated for tax evasion. Nellie had befriended Rhoda, charmed her into letting her guard down and leaking key facts that split the case open for both the paper and the police. Rhoda lost her job and faced charges herself until they found her dead from sleeping pills.

Helen shoved the tablet aside. "Well, this is just too much. If you're going to blame me for every action someone took after I said something or wrote something, we'll be here all night on this decade alone!"

The Bible flipped to Matthew 12: 36-37 *But I tell you that everyone will have to give account on the day of judgment for every empty word they have spoken. For by your words you will be acquitted, and by your words you will be condemned.*

Helen pointed her pen at the Bible as she answered back. "That's fine by me because I've written plenty of words that helped people! Feature stories on homelessness and child abuse. Op-ed pieces on the need for the government to end the war or to give women equal rights. My words have won awards!"

She flipped through the next pages of her autobiography reading phrases aloud:

"I graduated from Brown Summa Cum Laude. I was a feature reporter and assistant editor of the Brown Daily Herald."

"My early news articles did not garner much attention but as my skills grew, so did acknowledgment of my work through promotions, bylines, and awards."

"I am proud to say my reporting on the charity work of Newport socialites encouraged many to increase their charitable giving."

"While other women of my time were focused on finding a husband, the right floor wax, and bringing children into an already overpopulated world, I am proud to say that from 1952 to 1961, I made journalism my priority. Yes, I married your grandfather and yes, I gave birth to your Uncle CJ and your mother, but I wasn't defined by domestic pursuits."

Helen finished reading that chapter and stood, stretching and pacing to soothe her agitation. She looked at the citations on her shelves and walls. Moments. Memories. Accomplishments.

"I've lived with purpose. I've worked hard. I won't let you stain it all red just because I didn't mutter a few words that made your Son my *personal* Savior. That's crazy." She gestured as though God was sitting in the room. "You're going to judge every word? No one can stand up to that scrutiny. If that's your standard, then no one deserves heaven!"

Helen didn't know to whom she was talking to at this point but the faithful Bible flipped again. She tried to ignore it, even turned her back before curiosity snared her.

Romans 3:20 *Therefore no one will be declared righteous in God's sight by the works of the law; rather, through the law we become conscious of our sin.*

Helen pulled her shawl tighter and set her jaw. "I don't see what good it does me at all to be conscious of past sin. I can't go backward. There's nothing I can do about it now."

The phone rang and Helen turned, trying to locate where she had left it. Her hand trembled as she found it beneath a pillow on her chair.

"Hello?" she shouted into the receiver, undoubtedly giving the caller second thoughts about interrupting her silent night.

# Chapter Seven

"Ma, what gives? Ma? I need money."

Lizzie.

"Merry Christmas to you, too, Elizabeth." Helen rubbed her temple and stared out over the bay.

"Christmas? It's Christmas?" Lizzie sniffed into the phone. In the background, dishes clinked and people argued. "What time is it there? Are you on your second or third Irish coffee?"

Helen frowned and set her cup down on the desk. "I'm not drinking coffee. I came upstairs to find a book to settle a debate downstairs at the party," Helen said, glancing at the Bible.

"Okay, whatever. About the money."

"Don't waste any time on sentiment, Elizabeth. I'm only your mother and it's only Christmas," Helen said.

"When did you get sentimental? And when did you start caring about Christmas?" Lizzie sniffed again and a male voice called for her to hurry. "What was it you used to say to us? Religious holidays are excuses for lazy minds to indulge in sloth and football."

Helen glanced at the Bible again. "I don't remember ever saying that. From where are you calling?"

"A diner near the ashram. Picked up a few breakfast shifts to pay bills. I'm short, Ma, end of the year and all. Just a cash flow thing. Howard's in between gigs but he's got something lined up after the New Year. We need a boost until then. You have a pen?"

"I always have a pen."

"What was I thinking? Write down the address for Western Union over here. Just add it to the list. I'll head there after my shift."

"Again, Elizabeth. It's Christmas Eve here. Even if I do choose to wire you money, I cannot possibly do it before tomorrow." The nerve of this child.

"What about Paul or Nate? Have them go."

"Your nephew is in Afghanistan, Elizabeth. Please tell me you remember that much."

"Ease up, Ma. I meant to say, Harry. Like you said. It's Christmas. Don't you have any Christmas spirit?" The sound muffled for a moment as if Lizzie had covered the receiver with her hand.

"Elizabeth? Are you still there?"

The sound cleared. "Look, Ma, I'm not feeling too good. I need to see a doctor and the American ones are pricey here. I guess I could go to the free clinic, but I heard there's cholera going around." Lizzie sniffed again.

"You have no shame."

"Seriously. Can't we skip the preliminaries this once? This is what we do, you and I. I screw up. You send money. You feel superior. I leave you alone. If we don't have this, we've got nothing, right?"

"I wasn't mother of the year, Elizabeth, but I didn't raise you to beg. I raised you to use your mind. To be your own person."

"Well, my own person is broke and my mind is telling me to turn to my accomplished, well-heeled mother in my hour of need. Besides, you'd love it! I'm gaining insight over here, Ma. Eastern thinking has totally informed my perspective on life and …"

"Have you spoken with your children lately, Elizabeth?"

"The kids? Yeah, yeah, of course. I'm going to call them right after you. They're doing great in school and all. Winning all kinds of awards."

"You must be chatting with some other family, Elizabeth. Your children are struggling." Helen tapped her pen on the desk. "Gavin has Milo seeing a therapist. I didn't even know seven-year-olds experienced depression. Poppy is having nightmares and still sucking her thumb. The school calls Gavin every other day about Benson's outbursts. Last week he punched a little girl on the playground."

"Gavin or Benson?"

"I don't see anything to joke about here, Elizabeth. My grandchildren deserve better."

"Point taken, Ma. I'm a little out of touch. But, they're kids. Gavin's a model father and kids are resilient. You always said that, right? Besides, you weren't exactly doting, were you, Ma? You traveled. You never said no to a long "away" assignment. We turned out fine."

"Mmmm. When do you expect your spiritual adventure in India will come to a close, Elizabeth?"

A crash in the background like silverware spilling into a metal bin. A man shouted. "C'mon, Lizzie. Full tables!"

"Ma, I gotta go. I'll text Harry the address. Just send money, all right? A few grand will tide me over. You won't even miss it. I'll catch up with the kids later. You're a lifesaver, Ma, a lifesaver. Have another coffee on me and don't spare the whiskey."

Click.

*Well, that was touching.*

Helen stewed for fifteen minutes, pacing and replaying the call in her head, responding differently each time. She considered various ways to teach her self-centered daughter a lesson all the time knowing that in the end, she would simply send cash and await the next call.

She shook her head and stared at the coffee maker for a long moment before returning to the desk and flipping the page.

Of course. What a perfect chapter to follow that call.

"The Decade of Guns and Roses"

Where were you when Kennedy was shot? The question of her generation. Everyone had an answer. Except Helen. What Helen remembered was where she was supposed to have been. That's the scene she'd recorded.

Charles' voice was strained over the phone. "My brother met the train, Nel, but you weren't on it. Please tell me there was a mix-up."

"How is she, Charles?"

"How is she? Your two-year-old daughter is in intensive care fighting for her life, that's how she is! Where are you?" Charles' tone was uncharacteristically panicked. A grave sign.

Unsettling.

But no, children beat pneumonia every day.

"Please calm yourself, Charles. I was heading downstairs to catch a cab when news of the president came over the wire. You can't possibly expect me to leave Washington now."

"The president? Whatever story there is about the president will still be there tomorrow, Nel. I told you Kat may not survive the next few hours. What are you thinking?"

"Aren't there televisions at the hospital? How can you not have heard? The president's been shot." Nel was amazed at her husband's myopia. Always as if the hospital walls contained his whole world.

"Shot? No. I ... I haven't left her bedside except to make this call. How bad is it?"

"He's in surgery, but our sources say it's likely he won't make it." Now, he was finally understanding.

"I won't make it, either, Nel, not if you're telling me that you'd rather cover the president's death than to be here as our daughter verges on hers."

"You're being overly dramatic. You know I love Kat, but how can I possibly help her by sitting at her bedside wringing my hands? Is that the kind of wife you want?" Nel looked at a flurry of activity in the newsroom and felt her anxiety edge up. She couldn't miss the scoop on this headline. "Kat has her father beside her. Her father, who is one of the finest doctors in New England. I'm hardly deserting her to strangers in her hour of need."

"No? How about me, Nel? How about my hour of need? Has it occurred to you that I need you? What if she doesn't make it and I'm here .... alone?" His voice broke followed by a long silence.

The other reporters were reading feed off the wire. *Vultures*. Every instinct in her urged her feet to race to stand with them. She had to say something. Extricate herself from the call. "The staff at that hospital are like family to you. You've always said so. Certainly there's someone there who can hold your hand through this."

Silence.

*Think. Say something comforting. Get off the phone.*

"Besides, if Kat were dying, I would feel it. I'm a mother and my mother's instinct says she's going to pull through. She's like me, Charles; she's a fighter, right? You're an excellent doctor. You won't let one of your own children die."

"Nel," Charles' voice was a whisper. In the background, staff were paged and monitors beeped.

Beeping was good. They were beeping, not screaming, not whistling, not silent. Kat would pull through. The cluster of reporters scattered.

"Charles, I have to go. I'll catch the first train after I file my story. I promise. You'll see. She'll be fine. We'll be fine. Kiss her for me."

And she was. Helen was right. Katherine did pull through. What did a sick toddler know about the exact moment her mother reached her bedside? The story was filed as well as the follow-up stories. Helen made it home from DC after the funeral. Kat was sitting up eating solid food and Charles had found support. Her best friend, Jean Whitmore, was like a second mother to CJ and Kat after all.

Helen glared at the Bible on her desk. It was unmoving. "That's right," she said aloud. "You'd better not have anything to say about that! I didn't make any different choice than a male reporter would have. If I'm a sinner, so is every man!"

She wasn't sorry about that choice and had written that scene in her life story without apology so future generations would see the sacrifice she'd made to be a part of history. Her coverage of the funeral won local awards and got her noticed by influential people. Kat recovered and she wouldn't have healed any faster had Helen been by her bedside. There was only one significant negative side effect from that night.

Charles stopped sending her roses.

He'd sent the first bouquet the day after the incident with Monty and Vivian in the Salinger's foyer and he'd sent her one dozen red roses every week since. Always with a card that read simply, "Forever, your Charles."

But the week of the president's funeral passed with no delivery. She didn't notice until a week after she'd returned home and there was still no bouquet.

They didn't speak of it and she chalked it up as a form of male pouting, even when an entire year passed without roses. Then two. Then three.

But then, they were both very busy.

# Chapter Eight

No one who didn't live through the sixties can truly appreciate their complexity. Hippies. Free love. The Beatles. Vietnam. Civil Rights.

Charles almost missed it all. His world was medicine, his patients, Newport, and their two children. He passed up every career opportunity that might force him to relocate or to spend time away from home.

Nellie didn't miss a thing. Her world was the world. She prided herself on hiring competent staff capable of following her instructions on raising CJ and Kat so she could work late or chase a story across the country if necessary. The civil rights movement was her passion—and would prove to be her ethical Waterloo.

She was honest about that in her autobiography too. Journalism is a cutthroat field. Helen was cutthroat without regret. She stroked the page as she read on. These were exciting years. Life was a game and Nellie Bancroft a player.

Standing on the other side of Jim Daniel's desk, his door flung open, Nellie didn't care everyone could hear. She was more worried she would attempt to murder her chief editor with an office full of witnesses. "How can you even consider giving her that story? That's my story!"

Jim cleared his narrow little throat. "You can't be serious. If you were a reader, whose perspective would you want to read?"

"The best writer's."

"The best writer for this story is Season Hazard."

"Because she's black?"

"Because she's the right writer to cover the walk from Selma to Montgomery. Hands down, Nel."

"I've done all the background work. Those are my contacts. The movement is my beat. My interview with Dr. King won awards. I have five years here over her! You can't do this to me. It's discrimination!"

"Walk yourself out of my office right now, Nel, before you say something that'll force me to fire you."

"I made this paper."

"It's always about you, Nel. Have you noticed that? Look around! There's a team of people on this paper. You're just one cog in the machine." He pointed a stubby, ink-stained finger at her. "Now back out of this office while you still have a job and turn your notes over to Season by morning."

His office door slamming shook the entire news floor. Nel collided with Stony Brewster, the gopher gathering copy, and sent the pages flying.

"Tough break," Stony said as he bent to retrieve the articles.

"Stow it," Nel replied, but she joined him on the floor. No matter what, the news was sacred. As she crawled around, she paged through her options. She'd never let anyone take a story from her, never before, and she wasn't about to let it happen now.

After a moment, her hands full and her back to Stony, a terrible, wonderful idea occurred to her. She quite possibly held the answer to her problem in her neatly manicured hands.

Season Hazard's latest article was here in her grasp. Nel stared at it. Two brief pages. Nothing special. A fill piece on local politics. It could be perfect. Nel scanned the first paragraph.

Standard hook. Stock phrases. Rookie writing.

If Nel had written it, even as a rookie, it wouldn't be predictable. She'd have put a spin on it that turned fill into news.

Maybe she still could.

She thumbed through all the copy. Every story was on identical paper, indistinguishable except for the coffee stains on Murphy Malone's sports report. She could absolutely do this.

"Hey, Stony," Nel shoved all the papers but Season's article into the gopher's hands. "I just realized I forgot to change the hook on mine. I have time to fix it, right? If I walk it down myself?"

"Jeez, Nel, Jim'll be steamed if he sees me letting you do it. You know how he is about deadline." Stony glanced at the editor's office.

"Then, I'll have to work fast, won't I? Don't worry, kid, I'm a pro."

Nel dashed to her desk and flipped through her past files. There had to be an old story that was similar, one that would work.

There. Perfect. She yanked out a four-year-old file. This was going to be unbelievably easy. She mentally packed for Selma as she worked.

As other reporters left for the night, Nel hastily retyped Season's short piece exactly the way Season had written it except for one change. Rather than Season's lead, Nel inserted, word-for-word, the lead she'd written years ago on a similar piece—the first two paragraphs to be exact—from a previously published piece—that had her by-line.

When she finished, she whipped it from the carriage, relishing the clack of the wheel teeth, then shoved the original pages into her bag to dispose of at home. Pulling it off was as easy as dropping the altered copy onto the layout desk as she danced out the door for the night.

The rest was like stealing an assignment from a baby reporter who had yet to cut her canine teeth.

Nel waited an hour after arriving in the newsroom the next morning before knocking on Jim Daniel's door.

"What?" he called out.

Nel ignored the cigar smoke that made a permanent cloud in his office. She eased the door shut and tried to appear hesitant and nervous. Not an easy act for her to pull off.

"Well, what's your problem now, Bancroft? I told you my answer about Selma." Jim looked over the morning edition as he took great gulps of his black coffee from a thick, white mug.

"Look. I respect why you're sending Season to cover the march. I get it. But, I'm wondering if maybe you're pushing her too hard for someone so green." Nel looked out over the newsroom and saw Season chatting with Murphy by the coffee pot. She wore a new navy-blue suit today. Probably purchased it especially for the trip south.

Jim sat back in his chair and studied her before putting both hands behind his head. "All right. You've captured my curiosity. I'll bite. What makes you think I'm pushing her too hard and exactly why do you suddenly care?"

"I care when someone plagiarizes my work and so should you." With those words, she tossed the day's paper onto his desk, folded open to Season's piece. Then beside it, she laid a copy of her story, published four years prior.

"Plagiarizes? What are you talking about? She'd never—" Jim stopped talking as his eyes caught up with his thoughts. She noticed there wasn't much hair left beneath the swoop he combed from left to right as he glanced several times back and forth from one article to the next. "Well, I'll be hornswoggled. I never—"

Nel interrupted. "Look, Jim. I know what you're going to say. We're well aware of your stance on plagiarism and I, for one, respect it entirely, but I think you should go easy on the kid this time. With the pressure you put on her and all the prep she's probably been cramming for the march, who among us hasn't thought of taking a short cut once or twice?"

"I haven't. That's who. And neither have you! And neither will anyone who works for me, I'll tell you!" Jim's face was purple and his mouth moved in angry circles like a pit bull ready to bare his teeth. "I'm surprised at you, of all people, Nel, expecting me to go soft on her just because she's under pressure. That's what the news is about. We're always under pressure, but we don't cave, we don't plagiarize, and we don't take shortcuts! Not on my watch!"

Jim pushed away from his desk and shoved past Nel, opening the door. "Hazard!" He called out. "My office! Now!"

Nel saw a look of terror and confusion cross Season's face as Jim walked past her back to his desk. "And you," he said, pointing at Nel. "Pack your bags."

That's what it took in those days. A woman had to be as hard-hitting and as ready to fight dirty as any man. The stories she filed from Selma won her a place in the news business it would have taken years of society pieces for her to earn. This is an unforgiving world if people aren't willing to do whatever it takes to go after what they want. Nel was willing.

Helen was about to turn the page when the Bible she thought had entered sleep mode stirred and opened to a passage in 1 Timothy 6:6-9. Helen sighed and pulled the book closer. *But godliness with contentment is great gain. For we brought nothing into the world, and we can take nothing out of it. But if we have food and clothing, we will be content with that. Those who want to get rich fall into temptation and a trap and into many foolish and harmful desires that plunge people into ruin and destruction.*

"Well, that's where you have me all wrong, God," Helen said aloud. "Money? When did I ever want for money? Money has always been there for me. This wasn't about money. It was about ambition. It was about going after what I wanted. The money's a benefit. Don't get me wrong, but really, this was about me. It was all for me."

The Bible flipped again. This time to Philippians 2:3-4. *Do nothing out of selfish ambition or vain conceit. Rather, in humility value others above yourselves, not looking to your own interests but each of you to the interests of the others.*

"Well, that's preposterous. Now you sound like Kat and where has this type of thinking gotten that child in life?" Helen crossed her arms over her chest. "She's a fine mother, yes, and she keeps a lovely home, but she has no career, no mark in the world, no path of her own! No self-respecting woman operates that way in this world today, not if she's going places."

She leaned forward and tapped the pen on the table.

"I wasn't trying to be evil. It was my story. If Season had been good enough to compete, she'd have found a way to beat me and keep her job. I stole from her before she could steal from me." Helen saw the Bible flipping and tried to focus on the boat bobbing on the water, the tree lights lining its sail. Finally, she read the lit passage aloud. James 3:16 *For where you have envy and selfish ambition, there you find disorder and every evil practice.*

Helen pursed her lips. This wasn't fair. It's as if God didn't understand the rules of the world He created. But, if she was going to win this dare, she had to do it within the parameters laid out in the note.

"This Bible is full of lovely thoughts. These verses would make wonderful stitchings for parlor pillows, but no one on earth actually thinks we can live this way. Aren't you paying attention? No one obeys this. And if they do, they get trampled on by everyone else—like Season."

Reluctantly, Helen ran a red line through the story. As she did, her hand quivered slightly and she felt something stir within her. Something so new, she couldn't name it, but she wanted it to go away.

Just then, the tablet glowed and Season Hazard appeared on screen, sitting in a tasteful but sparse living room before a wood stove and a small Christmas tree. Around her knees were four small children. Standing beside her, a boy of about ten.

Helen waved a hand at the tablet. "Okay, stop now. If you're going to show me how my actions to steal the story and get Season fired ruined her life, I already get it. We can skip the visual."

But the scene played on.

The boy, wearing a sweater vest and tie, looked over Season's shoulder at a scrapbook on her lap. "Mommy, did you really get fired from that job? Did you do something that made your boss mad?" He pointed at a photo of Season standing in front of the news office smiling and holding her first published article.

"Yes, I was fired but it was nothing I did wrong, Simon. It was a dreadful mix-up. My boss accused me of copying someone else's story and pretending it was mine."

"Ooooh, that's bad. Teacher says we should never copy," said a little tyke with black ringlets.

"Teacher's right, Lydia. It is wrong to copy, but mommy was falsely accused. I was fired even though I was innocent."

The older boy frowned. "That's not fair. Weren't you mad? I would have been."

Season nodded. "Yes, I was most definitely angry for a long time but then your Aunt Star sat me down and reminded me of the story of Joseph in the Bible. Do you remember that story?"

The children nodded as Season continued. "Joseph's brothers sold him into slavery and Potiphar put Joseph in jail for many years even though he'd done nothing wrong. But it all happened because God had a plan for Joseph."

"Did God have a plan for you, Mommy?" asked Lydia.

"He certainly did. Mommy took all her anger and went back to school until she earned her doctorate of letters. God provided money through scholarships and that's how Mommy became the first black female professor at the University. God showed Mommy that He didn't just want her to tell the story of civil rights; He wanted her to be part of history. Mommy had a plan, but God had one that was much, much better. Don't you think?"

"Well, yeah," said Simon. "You made history and you met Daddy at the University, right? We wouldn't be here if you hadn't followed God's story, would we?"

The tablet went dark and Helen cocked her head to the left.

"I don't get it. You make me cross out my story because it's sin, but then you show me that my wrong choice, led Season into a better life than she would have had if I hadn't cheated her? Doesn't that make what I did a good thing?"

The tiresome Bible flipped again, this time to Romans 8:28. *And we know that in all things God works for the good of those who love him, who have been called according to his purpose.*

"Season loved you so you took my bad thing and made it turn into good for her? Something's sure off about that. What's so special about her? First, Jim picks Season over me and then you do, too?" Helen waved her hands around as if God was sitting across from her. "Well, that's a fine thank you. Don't you recognize people who work hard? People who know their stuff and show courage and dedication to reporting the truth? My writing made a difference in the way people saw the events in the South. It opened a lot of racist eyes. But, of course, you'd take her side. Her and all the other goody-two-shoes out there. So, fine, give her special help, but then you can't blame the rest of us for fending for ourselves!"

Helen slammed the Bible shut and flipped back through the chapter she'd just edited. If ambition and self-interest were sins, it was to be a very red decade with little story left to stand.

Seemed fitting, somehow.

The decade began with Kennedy's assassination and the end of her rose bouquets. Blood-red rage flowed relentlessly through the civil rights battle and continued until it fired through the barrels of the guns that killed Dr. King and then Bobby Kennedy.

June 5, 1968. That was the night she ran all the way to the downtown free clinic where Charles was volunteering carrying CJ as he bled profusely from a gash to his head. He'd been playing on a boat at the docks as she shopped for dinner when he slipped and fell onto the cobblestones headfirst.

And it was there, in the doorway of the clinic covered with her son's blood she discovered a betrayal that would alter the decade to come.

# Chapter Nine

"How could you, Jean? Honestly, how could you?" Nellie was breathless from running several blocks carrying CJ and from what she witnessed when she burst through the back entrance.

Jean stared at her as though she was the interloper. "Right now, I think we should focus on CJ, don't you, Helen? We can discuss everything else later."

How dare she act superior! "Oh, that's rich! Not only do I find you with your hands on my husband, but now you're going to stand there and act as if you care more about my children than I do!"

The other woman held up a hand as she glanced into the exam room where Charles worked on CJ "Those are your words, not mine, but you might want to ask yourself why I've attended more of their school events than you have."

"Maybe it's because I have my own life! I'm not lurking around town trying to steal someone else's!

Jean straightened magazines that were already straight as she paced around the tiny waiting room. "Do you ever think about what they need, Helen? Or Charles? Doesn't it even occur to you he has needs?"

Nellie put her hands up to cover her ears but realized they were smeared with CJ's blood. He cried out from the exam room and Nellie dashed to the window. A white-uniformed nurse was holding CJ in her lap as Charles threaded a needle. Nellie pulled away and turned back to Jean.

"You have no idea what you've done," she hissed.

Jean took a step closer and lowered her voice. "What makes you angriest, Helen? That your husband loves another woman or that your life is a cliché?"

Nellie backed away practically screaming, "Don't you say another word, Jean Whitmore! Not one more word, do you hear me, or you'll regret it!" CJ's cries sailed from the exam room.

Jean raised her volume, too. "The only thing I regret, Helen Bancroft, is that I haven't tried harder to convince Charles to leave you. You don't deserve a man like him and you sure don't deserve those two beautiful children."

That's when a terrible awareness dawned on Nellie. "Kat! Oh my goodness, I thought she was right behind us when we ran here!"

"You had Kat with you when this happened?" Jean's eyes widened at her words.

Nellie dashed for the door. "Tell Charles where I've gone. She's probably still at the store or waiting on the wharf."

Jean just stared.

"Don't look at me that way. CJ was hurt. Any mother would have focused on her injured child. I'm sure she's fine and you, of all people, ought to be thankful she didn't walk in when I did and see her father in the arms of another woman!"

Fortunately, Kat was on the curb just outside the store eating an apple from the sack beside Nellie's abandoned bag of groceries. When Nellie returned to the clinic, Jean was gone and the nurse informed her that Charles had taken CJ home. When she arrived at their house, the nanny was in with CJ and Charles was in their bedroom.

He stood with his back to her at the window. Nellie walked to their closet and pulled his suitcase from the top shelf. As she tossed it onto the bed, Charles turned to her. She looked at him long enough to notice he'd lost weight. His face was pale and drawn. Shocks of gray appeared just at his temples. She felt a tug in her midsection and put her arm there to brace herself. When he tried to hold her gaze, she turned away.

"Nel, we need to talk," he said.

"There's nothing to say, is there, Charles? You've made your choice. I want you out of here tonight."

"Nel, it's not ..."

She held up a hand and backed into the doorway. "Please. Don't make it worse by saying something pedestrian and banal like 'It isn't what you think.' or 'It didn't mean anything.' I couldn't bear it if we started to act out a scene from a lousy "B" roll movie. Bad enough you've cheated, don't bore me now, as well."

"No. No. I won't bore you with the facts, Nel. Or my feelings. Or my side of the story. You wouldn't want that, would you?"

The phone in her study rang and Nel looked down the hall.

"Go ahead," Charles said. "It's probably important."

By the time Nel returned, he had packed some of his things and left. That night, Sirhan Sirhan gunned down Bobby Kennedy and the next afternoon, Nel took the first flight she could book to California. When she arrived home, two weeks later, CJ was back to himself with only a scar to show for his fall and Charles had taken a studio apartment near the hospital.

A month later, Jean and her husband moved to Beacon Hill in Boston to be closer to his work (which was good since Nel ruined Jean's reputation locally with her whispered revenge). Nel and Charles developed a rhythm of spending time with the children without ever encountering one another, a rhythm that worked for over a year.

In the summer of '69, Charles started calling for her, leaving invitations to lunch. The children came home with notes from him asking her to meet. Until then, she'd managed to avoid being alone with him. When they were around the children together for holidays or birthdays, she kept the conversation civil but superficial. Charles was patient and she was busy. Mama Bea died so she and the children moved into the house on Sea View Avenue with Daddy. Still, she managed to keep their conversation to topics about the children or selling their house but she knew she couldn't put Charles off forever.

Neither of them contacted a lawyer, but it was on Nel's list of things to do. She'd been promoted to assistant editor and poured her attention and energy into proving herself the best.

One day in August, Nel was down two reporters when an office romance turned into a secret elopement. So when her best Arts and Entertainment reporter's mother died, she tried to convince him to get the family to postpone the funeral so he could cover a music festival on a farm in Upstate New York. He quit on the spot. Something about not wanting to work for a boss with no soul. Blah, blah, blah.

Nel had to cover the story. She'd finally agreed to meet Charles for drinks that Friday after work but canceled, leaving him a message that she had to drive to White Lake. After instructing Daddy's nurse and the nanny, she kissed the children good-bye and tossed her suitcase along with a packed cooler into her red Cadillac Deville convertible. Why she'd splurged on the convertible when she never took time to drive with the top down was a sore topic between Nel and the children. As she started the car, the passenger door opened and Charles slid in beside her.

"What are you doing?" she asked as he tossed his medical bag and an overnight tote into the back seat.

"I'm coming with you," he said, looking forward and settling into the seat.

"I'm on a story, Charles."

"And I'm on a mission, Nel. I'm not getting out of this car, so unless you want to miss this little concert of yours, we'd better hit the road."

They drove for hours listening to the radio and not talking. The drive should have taken a little under five hours, but the closer they got to White Lake, the more traffic they encountered. At first, Nel figured it was people heading out for the weekend, but eventually it became clear that the lines of cars filled with hippies and the trucks loaded with bell-bottomed adolescents were all headed to the same destination.

Charles, of course, was asleep but soon he was awakened by their lack of forward progress. The sun was setting and they were still miles from Yasgur's Farm, quickly becoming aware they were part of a strange parade of psychedelic pilgrims carrying guitars, babies, and duffle bags. Nel had never experienced a traffic jam that seemed more like a late night dorm party than a problem. Radios blared. Guitarists staged mini-concerts atop truck beds and car roofs. People shared food and weed from car to car. Before long, the radio announcer warned everyone hoping to reach the Woodstock concert that the roads were hopelessly jammed.

Nellie slammed her palm against the steering wheel. "That's just great. There's actually something worth reporting at this concert and I'm stuck in a car with you. It looks like you'll get your way after all. I'll turn around. We can talk somewhere over dinner on the way back to Newport."

Charles turned to her. "You're giving up?"

She pointed out her windshield, "Giving up? Look at it. People are actually leaving their cars in the road and walking. The sun'll be down soon. Some are camping roadside. And we're still miles from where it's really happening."

85

"That's just like you, Nellie," Charles said. "So focused on where you want to go, you miss the story happening right under your nose!" He rolled down his window and called out to a gang of hippies sitting on the embankment. "Hey, how far is it to the festival from here?"

"A few miles but you won't get through by car."

"Is there a motel nearby?"

"No way, man, but that's not what you want to do anyway. We're setting up to camp out under the stars, man! It's beautiful! You and your old lady should join us!"

"Mmph!" said Nellie. "Old lady, indeed."

"It's just a saying, Nel," Charles replied. "We need to find a place to pull over for the night."

"You can't be serious! You actually plan to sleep out on someone's lawn like a hobo?"

"For a reporter, Nel, you haven't got much sense of adventure."

Just then Nellie noticed a young white man running from vehicle to vehicle. He sported a huge red afro and rainbow suspenders. "What on earth?" she said. "Charles, roll up your window. He's probably looking for money."

Instead, Charles waved the young man over. "What do you need, son?"

"A doctor or a nurse. Someone who can help my old lady," he panted.

"Is she hurt?" asked Charles, reaching for his medical bag. "Has she taken any drugs?"

"No way, man, we're all natural. She's in labor and something's wrong. The baby's foot is coming out first!"

Charles glanced at Nellie, but she waved him on. As he hopped from the car, he called to the hippies on the side of the road, "Help my wife get the car parked, would you?"

86

Nellie marveled at the authority of his black bag as the longhaired crew hopped up and directed traffic until she was safely situated. Then, she grabbed her camera, slung her work bag over her shoulder and jogged down the road to the back of the VW van into which Charles had disappeared.

She found Charles with his hands inside a young woman in her twenties with long straight brown hair and stars painted on her face as she lay screaming on a pile of blankets. The red-haired man with the afro was beside her and watching from the front seat was a young brown-haired girl of four and a red-haired boy about two. The woman's screams were nearly impossible to bear.

"What can I do, Charles? Should I take the children outside?" she asked.

"No," the woman and her husband replied as one. The husband explained, "Soliloquy and Asterisk need to be here. Starshine and I believe that a family unit experiences life together and that is where we find our strength, right kids?"

The urchins nodded but hid their faces when Starshine screamed again. Nellie whispered into Charles' ear, "Should I try to get help?"

"No. Just keep everyone calm. I have the baby nearly turned."

Nel marveled at her husband's composure and skill. She rarely saw him work. She turned to the young man. "Do you mind if I take some photos? Um, I'm sorry; I don't know your name."

"Oh, yeah," He held out a hand, "I'm Floyd, Pink Floyd, but everyone calls me Floyd for short. And sure, take pictures. We're open to whatever the universe brings to us and today she's brought us you."

Nel was so focused on taking photos she was caught off guard when little Sweetwater Goldfarb's first cries filled the van with cheers and sighs of relief. As the family nestled to sing a group lullaby to their newest addition, Charles and Nel stepped into the starry night to look for a place to rest.

A hefty boy with bad acne accosted them. "Hey, you're a doctor, right? My friend's having a bad trip, man. Can you help?" Charles looked at Nel, who shrugged, then nodded. They found themselves occupied all night and most of the next day, Charles with his black bag, tending to the sick and Nel with her camera, taking photos and notes along the road as they made their way closer to the concert one patient, one story at a time.

Finally, late Sunday night, weary of hippies, mudslides, and lectures on dropping acid, the two took refuge in an abandoned tent on the concert grounds. They flopped onto their backs and lay still in the dark listening to Crosby, Stills, and Nash perform their set. After several long moments, Nellie spoke, "Charles, what you said about me being so focused on where I'm going that I miss the story right under my nose? You're right about that."

He was silent for a long moment before Charles replied, "I'm right about a lot of things, Nellie. But I don't want to be right. I want you."

He reached for her and they made love in a stranger's tent on Yasgur's farm as Crosby, Stills, and Nash sang "You Don't Have to Cry" to the muddy crowds. Later that day, they drove all the way back to Newport with the top down.

Charles moved in with them the next week and nine months later, they welcomed Elizabeth Guinevere Bancroft into the world. "Our Woodstock baby," as Kat was fond of telling everyone. A week after her birth, Charles sent Nellie a bouquet of red roses and they never stopped coming again until he died.

Helen set her pen down and stretched both arms out in front her, moving her neck from side to side. "There," she said aloud. "That should merit me some good that doesn't need to be red-penned! I assisted Charles tending to the medical needs of dozens of hippies at that mud-fest. I forgave him and kept our family together despite his unfaithfulness. Some would say that qualifies me for sainthood."

The computer sprang to life and Helen heard waiting room music like the type they used to pipe into the free clinic lobby. *What now?* She thought as she closed her eyes and tried to resist looking but finally glanced down.

Charles and Jean talking. Charles in his white coat. Jean, in that orange mini-skirt and tight cream-colored sweater, her blonde hair in a stiff beehive, her hand on Charles' arm. "Please, Charles, won't you even consider what I'm asking?"

"What you're asking is impossible, Jean. We're married. We both have families, commitments, and still some integrity."

"Integrity. Is that what you call it? Is that what keeps you from ever crossing the line and touching me? Holding me? Making love to me?" Jean stepped forward but Charles turned his back.

"You need to go home, Jean."

"There's nothing for me at home. You know that. He's not there for me and Helen is never there for you. Why won't you accept that? Why won't you acknowledge what you feel for me?"

Now Charles turned and took Jean's shoulders in either hand, ducking his head to look her straight in the eyes. "Jean, listen to me. You've been there for me through so much and you've helped me with the children—as a friend. But that's all you are to me, Jean, a friend. I love Nel and I made her a promise before God."

"She made promises to you, too, Charles but she's not the one standing by your side, I am."

"And that's been my mistake."

Jean's eyes filled with tears. "What do you mean, your mistake?"

"I never meant to lead you on. I see now that leaning on our friendship has given you the impression that I wanted more."

"You do want more, Charles. I see it in your eyes. I feel it when you're near me. I know she doesn't make you happy and I know that I can. Tell me she makes you happy and I'll walk away now."

Charles shook his head. "I can't tell you that. I'm not happy, but that doesn't mean I should spread that unhappiness to my children, to you, to Nick ..."

"Nick has been unfaithful since our first month together. There've been so many others, I've lost count," she sobbed. "I just want this one chance at happiness, Charles, please, please give me this chance." She moved into Charles' arms and buried her face in his chest.

Charles closed his eyes and patted her back but whispered, "I'm sorry, Jean. I love my wife and always will. I won't be unfaithful."

Just then, the two looked up as Nellie burst through the clinic doors carrying a bleeding CJ and the computer went dark.

Helen stared at the screen unmoving, eyes wide, overflowing with warm, fat tears. *No. No. No.* The only coherent word her mind would form. *No.*

Her body felt like it was on fire. It was hard to catch her breath. She trembled as if she was cold, but all she could feel was the heat. Heat like anger, like confusion, like horror and shame.

"It's not true." She slammed a fist on the desk like a gavel making her coffee cup hop and leap onto the floor, breaking into large wet pieces on the carpet, scaring the cat and splashing coffee onto the desk.

"Oh, look what you've made me do! This is foolishness. Absolute rubbish and I won't participate in it any longer." Helen stood trembling and crying and made her way to the bathroom down the hall. After splashing water on her face, she cleaned up the coffee mess and sat on edge of the overstuffed chair steadying herself. Gatsby jumped into her lap and she held him, stroking his fur as she closed her eyes, listening to him breathe.

"Harry. I need to talk with Harry," she whispered. "Find out how he arranged all this. Where he came up with these videos, this trick Bible, this crazy computer."

She pressed his number on speed dial.

"Gran, you okay?" Harry whispered. Music blared in the background.

"I'm sorry, Harry. I have to ask you about the gift you sent." Her voice sounded tight.

"Hold on. Mom's staring daggers at me. Let me get outside." Muffled sounds as she imagined he walked down the aisle to the door of the foyer. "Okay, what? Something about a gift?"

"The package you sent, Harry. The one with the fountain pen and the trick Bible. How does it work? Tell me how you've done this."

"I don't know what you're talking about, Gran. I wasn't planning to give you your present until tomorrow and it's not a pen. What's going on there?"

Helen squeezed her eyes shut. If it wasn't from Harry, was this something truly from God? Is it possible Charles hadn't been unfaithful? That she'd made him suffer so terribly because of her own stubborn assumptions?

"Gran? You're scaring me. How many Irish coffees have you had?" Harry asked.

"Never mind that. I …. I'm fine. I received a gift with no name on the card and I thought it must be from you, that's all. I'm sorry I interrupted the service."

"I should come home and check on you. You don't sound like yourself."

"No, no, your mother would kill me if I stole you away. I promise I'm fine. I'll see you when you get home."

"O-okay, but call me if anything strange happens."

She ended the call thinking there couldn't be anything stranger than what was already happening. Helen returned to her desk but rather than pick up the pen, she picked up the framed photo of Charles taken at his graduation from medical school. "I'm so sorry, my love. I'm so, so sorry. I didn't know."

91

She looked at the manuscript and then spoke to the Bible. "I don't know if I can keep at this. You know that my red pen deeds get so much worse."

# Chapter Ten

Nellie was no quitter. She sniffed and checked her reflection in the window. There were major red pen issues ahead but with four decades remaining, there was certainly enough good to redeem herself and win her bet. She straightened her back, blew her nose, and began again.

"The Best of Times." That was the confident title she'd bestowed on the decade spanning 1971 through 1980 and that was exactly how she remembered it. These were the best years of her life. Sally Field was a flying nun, Arnold Schwarzenegger pumped iron and Michael Jackson was still—well, recognizable.

It was a decade of headlines and as chief editor Nellie surfed every wave of news cycles from Kent State to the Munich Olympics, the Jason Foreman kidnapping to Jonestown. She directed most action from behind a desk, but her personal coverage of the deaths of ten female students in a Providence College dorm fire earned her accolades. Her first-person account of losing her father from complications following the Swine flu vaccination were revolutionary in moving local journalism to a deeper level of first-person reporting.

Charles was well respected and active in local philanthropy. The pair were never closer than they were in those years, enjoying a companionship that placed them in demand at social events. CJ and Kat were achieving in their private schools and Lizzie was an easy baby who grew into an easy child, her early years no foreshadow of the ones to come. Nellie, who by then was known primarily as Helen both personally and professionally, enjoyed her children. She outsourced the daily routine of their lives to well-vetted help but made a point of having dinner with them every Thursday night she was in town.

During these dinners, she quizzed them on current events and their studies. They gave her answers she wanted to hear and didn't venture information about CJ's experiments with hallucinogenic drugs or Kat's near-tragic first love affair with her English teacher. Helen would spend the seventies blissfully unaware of the dangerous riptide coming that would drag her family under in the decade ahead.

The years that followed tore tread marks on the lawn of their family history so here, in her story in the decade before it unraveled, Helen deliberately recorded one positive memory of each child and another that exhibited her devotion to them. First, for CJ.

Once a son reaches adolescence, he doesn't easily share tender moments with his mother. It takes illness or crisis to bring them together and Helen held two vivid memories of Charles Jr involving both.

"Mom, I'm so sick," CJ stood at her bedroom door wrapped in his football bedspread despite the fact that it was mid-July. "Can I come in with you?"

Helen could barely lift her own head off the pillow. This summer virus downed half the newsroom so she had tried to push through it. Today, though, Charles had threatened if she didn't remain in bed, he'd quarantine the newsroom. She waved CJ in, reaching for a tissue.

"What are you watching?" he asked, snuggling up. He would turn fourteen in September. She knew by the end of August every trace of little boy would disappear and he'd be all arms, legs, and acne. She smiled at the top of his head that hadn't changed through the years as she kissed him and tucked the covers around him.

"The Watergate trials. Are they explaining Watergate to you at school?" She smoothed his brown bangs out of his eyes.

"It's summer, mom. Boy, you really are sick!" He sneezed.

Summer. Right. Kat was at boarding camp where CJ would head when he was well. His summer had been delayed by testing for academic placement at his new high school.

"I'll tell you what. I'll ring for Maggie to bring us both some chicken soup, Saltines, and ginger ale while I educate you on the scandal that is Watergate."

"Mom, I'm sick. Now I have to learn stuff?"

"What if I told you it involved real life spies?"

"Like James Bond?"

"Well, less handsome and not as smart."

"Is there anything that happens in the world that you don't know about, Mom?"

"Not much."

They passed the day discussing the hearings and power. She taught him to play poker. By evening, Charles declared CJ well enough to come to the dinner table. Helen felt the emptiness of his departure long into the night.

Flash forward. CJ's last summer before Dartmouth. He had the same look he had at thirteen standing at her bedroom door only now he's nearly a man knocking on her office door at the paper.

"Mom, I'm in a bit of trouble." His brown eyes, so like Charles', threatened to penetrate her tough work exterior, but she refused to yield.

She couldn't afford to soften behind this desk.

"Can it wait until tonight?"

CJ stepped into the office and closed her door. Stared at the top of her desk chewing his bottom lip. "Mom …"

She set her pen on her notepad. "All right. It's serious. You'd best come out with it."

"It's Martha Rose."

Helen sighed. "We've been over this, Charles Jr. She's welcome to come to the family dinner, but you will not be spending your last night at home running around with your girlfriend! It's not proper. The two of you aren't even engaged. Do I need to have a chat with her?"

"She's pregnant."

Helen glanced at the staff working on the other side of the window. She focused her gaze on the smiley face stickers plastered on corkboard outside the perky intern's cubicle. She despised those stickers.

"Mom. Did you hear me? Martha Rose is going to have—"

"I heard you." She looked squarely at CJ He was going to need new shirts for Dartmouth. His were too tight in the shoulders. "What do you need? Is she asking for money? A ride to the clinic? Whatever it is, I'll arrange it. No one will know. Especially not your father." Helen penciled notes on a legal pad. Calls she would have to make.

"No, Mom. I … we … we want to do the right thing. We want to get married. I'll put off college for now. Get a job. I … need your help telling Dad."

Helen's head snapped up and she glared at her son. "That is not what's going to happen here. Your father and I have a plan for you. We've set you on a course and that course passes through Dartmouth not through a rushed wedding and a job beneath your capabilities and intellect." Helen picked up the phone and dialed.

CJ stepped forward. "Mom? We need to discuss this."

She held a hand up to silence him. "Hello? Yes. Martha Rose? This is Helen, CJ's mother. Let's you and I have lunch today at Tula's. Yes? Perfect. I'll meet you there at noon."

"Mom," CJ protested but she set her face and, she imagined, he'd seen the look enough times to know it was no use to argue.

"Go home. Your father left a list of errands for you today."

"Mom?"

"It's done, CJ. Go home."

She settled the whole business with one lunch conversation, a check, and hired car to Boston. No one else ever knew except one discreet driver. By the following summer, Martha Rose was dating a boy she'd met at Brown and CJ, well, CJ had found a new way to screw up his life, one Helen couldn't fix with a telethon of phone calls.

Her sweetest memory of the girls happened during the Blizzard of '78. Helen had taken a rare day off from the paper to complete a freelance editing project at home. Kat, nearly seventeen, and Lizzie, eight, were released early from school. Charles phoned to say he'd be sleeping at the hospital in case the storm blocked the roads. When the pace of the snow picked up in the afternoon, Helen generously allowed the help to leave early, figuring she and the girls could fend for themselves for one night.

But it was four nights and five days before they had contact with anyone else. The blizzard dumped almost thirty inches of snow on Rhode Island cutting off power and blocking roads for days. Helen and the girls set up camp in the same living room where Helen had awoken years earlier to news of AJ's death at Pearl Harbor. They kept a fire burning and ate peanut butter sandwiches and hotdogs they roasted on grilling forks, read, played games, and told stories by firelight.

"Momma, tell us again how Daddy proposed to you in New York City," Lizzie begged the second night as she lay wrapped up in Momma Bea's old goose-down quilt.

"Mm, I love that story, too, Momma. What was the name of that hotel where you stayed? The Carlyle, wasn't it?" Kat said. She was stitching patches on her bellbottoms, a fashion trend that appalled Helen.

She sighed. "Why, may I ask, do my two daughters, who are being raised in the Age of Aquarius to be strong, equal, independent women, only want to hear stories about my romantic life? You never ask me for stories about my work as a reporter." Helen huddled beneath a quilt her older sister had given her as a wedding gift, created from scraps of the dresses Momma Bea had sewn over the years.

"The reporter stories are boring, that's why!" Lizzie moaned.

Kat waved her hand as if to swat Helen's question away. "We live with the reporter every day, Mommy-o! I don't want to read the newspaper; I want to be with you! Your work is only one part of your life; it's not everything, is it?"

Kat's question stirred something in Helen. She wasn't sure if she was flattered by the observation or worried. She realized it had been a long time since she'd had their full attention.

"I know, why don't I tell you stories about the life I had growing up in this house?"

"Back in Roman times, you mean?" Lizzie teased and Kat giggled.

Helen threw pillows at them but then settled in for hours of family history the girls absorbed like sponges. Even with the inconvenience of no electricity, Helen relished the rare opportunity to connect, especially with Kat.

By the summer of '78, Kat was a changed girl. That was when she found Jesus after a production of some propaganda film called *A Distant Thunder*. A dreadful movie created by fundamentalist

Christians to scare innocent teens into conversions, which is precisely what happened the night Kat's friend brought her to the theater. Helen was horrified, but Charles talked her into humoring Kat for fear she'd run off and join a cult like many of their friends' children had.

"Mom," Kat explained as she sat weeping on her bed late one night. "I just wish you would understand how real this is and how serious I am about Jesus."

Helen stood in the doorway. "There's nothing wrong with a little religion, Kat. Your grandfather prayed and went to church. I just don't want you becoming a fanatic."

"What is that supposed to mean?" Kat asked.

"All of this is so unnecessary." Helen indicated Kat's walls, which she'd plastered with Jesus posters and Bible verses written on index cards. "You read that Bible every day and I heard from Murphy Malone you were handing out tracts downtown last Saturday. It's embarrassing."

The crushed expression on Kat's face stayed in her memory for a long time, but Helen always spoke her mind and wasn't about to stop now.

"I should have figured you wouldn't understand, Mother. I'm sorry my enthusiasm for Jesus is an embarrassment to you, but soon enough I'll be off at college and we won't have to cross paths."

"Kat." Helen took a step toward her, but Kat rushed past her down the hallway into the bathroom. The door slammed at a volume familiar to Helen. She heard it quite often that summer.

Helen glanced up from her editing and spoke to the Bible. "I'm sure asking Kat to tone down her Jesus campaign falls into the red line category, but I thought you were supposed bring peace on earth. That's not exactly the result you had in our house, is it?"

The pages of the Bible turned. "Seriously?" she said. "Have you got an answer for everything?"

There it was. Matthew 10:34-36, *Do not think that I have come to bring peace to the earth. I have not come to bring peace, but a sword. For I have come to set a man against his father, and a daughter against her mother, and a daughter-in-law against her mother-in-law. And a person's enemies will be those of his own household.*

"Wow," Helen remarked aloud. "At least you're honest. That's exactly what you did in our house. Well, between Kat and me, anyway. And Kat and Lizzie."

For the first time that night, Helen kept reading beyond the highlighted verses to verse 37-39. *Whoever loves father or mother more than me is not worthy of me, and whoever loves son or daughter more than me is not worthy of me. And whoever does not take his cross and follow me is not worthy of me. Whoever finds his life will lose it, and whoever loses his life for my sake will find it.*

Well, she thought, my life is certainly being lost in a sea of red tonight! I don't see how this losing, though, is going to help me find anything.

Helen turned back to finish the chapter with her final story, the one that showed her devotion to Lizzie. By 1981, Kat and CJ were off at college and Lizzie was fairly independent. The older children accused Charles and Helen of lightening up on their youngest and the truth was, between experience and parenting fatigue, they did. But Helen wasn't ready to give up control over her baby's life entirely.

"No, absolutely not. I forbid it." Helen stood now in Lizzie's doorway with her arms crossed. Lizzie stood across from her braced for a brawl, her hair in a silly ponytail that erupted from the top of her head, her oversized t-shirt hanging off one shoulder, and a neon pink pair of those foolish leg warmers over some kind of shiny, skin-tight capris.

"You can't forbid love, mother!" Lizzie screamed.

"Oh, yeah! You just watch me," Helen shouted back.

Charles came down the hallway and stood just outside the door. "What's all the screaming?"

"Your wife is prejudiced against black people, that's what!" Lizzie cried out as she flopped on her bed in dramatic fashion.

"Me! Prejudiced! I'll have you know, young lady, that I covered the march from Selma to Montgomery. I am most definitely not prejudiced." Helen drew herself up tall, indignant at the accusation.

"But have you ever soul-kissed a young black man, mother? Have you ever felt your pale white skin wrapped inside strong, black arms? Have you?" Lizzie sat up and screamed back.

"Have you?" Charles and Helen asked as one.

"Argh! You two make me crazy! You live in a bourgeois fascist bubble protected by power and money, but you have no context for understanding how the rest of the world lives."

"Big words from a child with a poster of Shaun Cassidy on her wall," Helen grumbled.

"I'm sorry. Would you be kind enough to explain to your bourgeois, fascist father what sparked this discussion?" Charles was still hoping to reach détente.

"Leon Evans," Helen and Lizzie answered in unison.

"Little Leon? That kid who's been hanging out at our house since kindergarten?" Charles seemed genuinely confused and Helen noticed how his hair was growing grayer by the day.

"Little Leon is apparently the soul-kissing black man who popped up earlier in our discussion," Helen said, waiting for that sink in.

It didn't take long. "Wait a minute," Charles replied, "Leon and Lizzie? You mean? But they're children."

"Daddy! I'm not a little girl anymore. I'm nearly a woman and Leon and I share a love that crosses racial barriers."

"Well, what it doesn't cross is this parental barrier, Elizabeth," said Helen. "You are not permitted to date yet and when you are, it will certainly not be Leon."

"Times are changing, Mom!"

"Well, let me know when times change so much that you can afford to move out, get your own home, and make your own rules, Missy, because until then, Leon is not welcome in our home."

"Daddy!" Lizzie turned to Charles.

"We'll discuss it another time, Elizabeth. But, I do agree you're too young to be kissing anyone, so your mother's ruling stands."

That battle wasn't won by parental declaration that night. It took many nights of locking Lizzie in her room and heated arguments followed, finally, by a visit to Leon's family. Once Helen explained to them that Lizzie was emotionally unstable and couldn't possibly love their son, he no longer tried to visit their home.

"The lengths I went to look out for those children's interests," she said aloud. Certainly, my commitment to them should count in my favor. No matter how things eventually turned out."

She completed her chapter with a conversation she had with Charles over a rare late night dinner.

"I wasn't prepared for Lizzie to turn into one of those door-slamming, angry teens I see at the clinic," Charles said as he spooned fried rice out of a take-out container.

Helen snapped her chopsticks apart. "Both girls baffle me. Lizzie with her defiance and insistence that we don't understand her generation and Kat with this cult-like fascination she has with Jesus! Did I tell you she wants to spend the summer on some missionary trip to France?"

"France? Who's she trying to convert in France? Didn't they know Jesus before we did?"

Helen waved her hands as if to say, "Exactly!"

They ate in silence for a minute before she sighed. "Well, at least we know CJ has his head on straight."

Charles nodded. "Yes, yes. He's doing fine. His studies are solid. Julie's a down-to-earth young woman. When we had dinner in November, he laid out his plan for life after graduation. Seemed very sound."

"That's a good thing," Helen sighed. "I'm putting all my hopes into our firstborn. At least we've done something right."

# Chapter Eleven

"The Black Hole."

This decade was a short chapter.

Maybe if she lived into her hundreds, Helen would emerge from the pain of these years with enough clarity to write more details but not yet.

It began with phone calls in the night.

Ring.

"Hello?"

"Mom, put Dad on the phone. I've been arrested."

"CJ? What? What's happened?"

"Just get Dad, all right, Mom?"

Ring.

"Hello?"

"Mom, I'm sorry. I need Dad again. I'm in Boston. In jail."

Ring.

"Mom, I'm staying at Ellen's for the night."

"I don't believe you, Lizzie."

"It's the truth this time, Mom. Honest."

"Fine, put Mrs. Snyder on the phone."

"She's not home."

"Put Ellen on the phone."

"She's not feeling well."

"Elizabeth, come home."

"I can't help that you never believe me. I'll be home tomorrow, maybe. I hate you."

Ring.

"Hello?"

"Mrs. Bancroft? Your son has left the rehab facility against our advice. I'm just calling to let you know we aren't responsible for him now."

Ring.

"Mom? It's Kat. Don't go crazy but we've eloped."

"Eloped? Why? Don't you want a real wedding? Wait, are you pregnant?"

"No, I'm not pregnant. Seriously, Mom, Paul and I know the strain you're under with CJ so we didn't want to make a big deal."

"You're too young to marry, Kat. You've barely finished your education. Traveled. Come home, we can have it annulled. We can fix this."

"Stop, Mom. There's nothing to fix. Paul and I belong together. And we've been called to the mission field, probably medical missions in Kenya."

"Called? Called by whom?"

"By God, Mom. Look, we'll visit in a month or so before we leave for our training. Kiss Daddy for me."

"Surely we should throw a reception—something?"

"You have your hands full. Paul's parents are taking wonderful care of us. Focus on CJ."

Ring.

"Mom? I screwed up big this time, Mom. I'm really scared. There are snakes everywhere and a guy outside is waiting to kill me."

"CJ, where are you?"

"I'm not sure. My friend has a place outside of Providence and we crashed here, but the snakes are everywhere, Mom. Please, help me!"

Three years of late night calls, long drives to jails, courthouses, and strange neighborhoods followed by hours in hospital waiting rooms, rehab facilities with molded plastic chairs and posters on the walls listing signs to watch for—signs they'd clearly already missed. Three years of crying into phone receivers, pleading yelling, negotiating. "Please, just tell us where you are now." "Please, come home and let us help you." "Please, return to the center." "What do you need?" "What can we do?" *When will this end?*

Helen staring at other dazed parents across visiting rooms where no one spoke unless it was their turn. Other parents whose children, like CJ, had tossed away educations, careers, opportunities, talents, and relationships, for pot, acid, speed, or heroin and who now spent hours learning to express their feelings using "I" statements and setting boundaries guided by "tough love."

Watching the other parents, she tried to tell herself that she and Charles were different but then CJ, pockmarked and rail-thin, was slouched in a plastic seat beside them, his knee bouncing, smoking an endless succession of cigarettes and repeating whatever mantra was the therapeutic slogan du jour at that facility.

CJ fell down a rabbit hole and she and Charles pursued him there. Rescuing him became a full-time endeavor while the newspaper and raising Lizzie were things she did around the margins of interventions and treatments.

By Christmas of 1982, poorer, humbler, and exhausted, they climbed out of the rabbit hole, victorious. CJ came back to them from the final facility clean, sober, and determined to make restitution by reclaiming the life he'd injected into his veins and inhaled through rolled up dollar bills.

He moved home and took classes at Brown to complete his degree while he honed his résumé. They solved the problem of Lizzie by setting her up in a Swiss boarding school far from the rapidly degenerating American youth culture that was turning her against them. She still hated them, but she was safe. They were relieved of the daily bouts of door slamming and name-calling reserved now for holiday visits.

Charles talked about slowing down and Helen dreamed about writing full-time. She took on freelance editing projects and hinted to the paper she was ready to make adjustments in her schedule. So, when Charles and CJ planned a father-son mountain climbing trip for August, Helen supported it whole-heartedly.

The three of them discussed it over dinner one January night as if they were a normal family.

"I think it's a perfect idea. I've been itching to try another peak since Mt. Shasta back in '78. Do you remember that one, Nellie? I hiked it with Wallis Tate from Urology." Charles took a mouthful of salad.

She smiled. "After the medical convention, right? How can I forget? You whip out the slides whenever we have guests who make the mistake of mentioning they haven't seen the photos."

Charles blushed and CJ laughed. "I hate that I missed out on that one. How many have we done together now, Dad? Three or four?"

Charles counted on his fingers. "Mt. Katahdin when you were fourteen. Mt. Washington when you were sixteen."

"Longs Peak when I was seventeen and Mt. Rainier for my nineteenth birthday."

"Denali, though," said Helen as she sliced her steak. "Will you both be up for it by August?"

"I've never been in better shape, Mom. Hours in the workout room at Pine Grove were required therapy." CJ buttered his roll.

"I'm more concerned about your father," she said.

"Me? I am a model of fitness and health," Charles said as he stopped mid-bite.

"For a man your age," Helen countered.

"My age! My age! I am perfectly healthy and I can still out-lift the younger men at the gym, I'll have you know." Charles stared wild-eyed at her as if she'd insinuated he was ready for a walker and a life alert necklace. "My age. I'll show you my age." He pushed away from the table and theatrically slid back her chair, snatched her by the wrist and lifted her into his arms.

"What are you doing? Put me down!" she said as her napkin floated to the floor.

"I will not. We're ascending to our room where I'm going to put discussion of my age to rest for the night." Charles turned toward the stairs as CJ moaned and waved his hands.

"Okay, way too much information. This is not a scenario I can handle on a full stomach." He rose from the table and grabbed his jacket and keys. "I'll be at the gym."

"Good!" called Charles as he climbed the stairs with her in his arms. "Because we plan to be very loud and quite athletic."

She swatted his shoulder. "Oh my goodness! Stop this nonsense now." But as they reached the top stair, she'd decided she enjoyed his show of masculine prowess and felt her heart race faster as the bedroom door closed behind them.

By the time her two men left for Alaska in August, her new study was ready. She was so eager to be alone with her thoughts, her projects, her words, that she didn't see them off at the airport. Instead, her final conversation was a rushed farewell as she leaned in to kiss them each goodbye through the window of the hired limousine.

"We'll call when we arrive, Nellie, but we won't have means of contact once we start the trek," Charles said as he felt his pockets for the tickets and his cash.

"I won't be sitting here wringing my hands. You're perfectly capable men. I'm sure you'll take care of one another." She pecked CJ on the cheek and then walked to Charles' window. As she kissed him one last time, she pointed at her son and warned Charles, "Just bring this one back unbroken and ready to start his new job after Labor Day. If you let anything happen to mess that up, Alaska will feel like the tropics compared to the chilly reception you'll get here!"

"I promise. We'll come back in one piece—actually, we'll be more whole than we are now," Charles said as he brushed her hair from her face.

"Love you, Mom," called CJ

"Yes, yes. Such a fuss over a little trip! Go on, now! I'm eager to be rid of you both."

She hadn't said she loved him, too. That wasn't a sin in God's book, she suspected, but she would never forgive herself for that omission. Never.

In red pen, Helen added it to her manuscript. "I love you too, Charles Jr. I love you too."

August 15.

An early morning phone call.

A stranger's voice. Alaskan state trooper.

A climbing accident.

A plane ride alone.

And Charles. Unconscious. Tubes, wires, monitors.

A woman surgeon explaining things she couldn't hear. Details that didn't matter.

A cold room. The morgue. Metal and shadows and antiseptic like peppermint candy.

A quiet doctor peeling back a sheet; a young man's face.

A scruffy face, as if he hadn't shaved in days. As if he had chosen to live untamed for three weeks before donning the new suit and tie that would now be his final garment.

Air. Air left her lungs, the room, the planet.

And the black hole that opened up swallowed the rest of the details.

Helen turned the page and held her breath knowing what would happen next. She had written no more in her manuscript, but the cursed tablet would have more to show about that decade. She just knew it, the years she couldn't put into words, the memories she couldn't face, the choices she tried to blot out of her own history still remained on record somewhere she was sure.

There. Of course. It glowed.

Helen gripped the head of her cane and sat upright in her chair staring out into the black night. She could hear, but she didn't have to watch.

Katherine's voice. "Mom, you can't be serious. Please, Paul and I are here to pay our respects."

Then Helen's voice, only not Helen's voice, the voice of a stranger echoing from inside a black hole. "I was very clear on the phone, Katherine. You're not welcome here."

"Where's Daddy? Get him. He'll let me in. Paul, do something."

"Your father is very fragile, too fragile to deal with this."

"But Mom, he was my brother. Please. We've flown all this way to be here; to see him one last time."

Paul's voice. "Helen, be reasonable."

"I am being reasonable. Katherine told me clearly some months ago that she was worried for Charles Jr's soul if he didn't become a Christian. Well, he didn't and I won't have anyone at this funeral who is thinking that my son is now in hell."

"Mom, I'm not here to cause a problem. I just want to grieve with everyone else."

"If you think a loving God would lock your brother out of heaven, you'll have no problem believing a loving mother would lock you out of this service. Now, please leave or I'll call the police."

"Mom!"

Helen closed her eyes and squeezed her face at the sound of Katherine's cries as the door to the funeral home closed her out.

The screen flickered to a new screen.

"It was my fault." Helen didn't have to look at the tablet to recognize Charles' voice, to remember his confession, to know they were sitting in Dr. Jacoby's office—grief therapist, marriage counselor, voodoo doctor for all it mattered.

"It's normal to feel that way, Charles," Dr. Jacoby's British accent gave him an added air of authority, pomposity if you asked Helen.

"It's normal because it's true," Helen's voice, that strange Helen, announced from the tablet.

"You blame your husband for your son's death, Helen?" Dr. Jacoby.

"He didn't secure the belay. It's in the report. It's fact. He caused the death of my son and the other man, their guide. He feels responsible because he is responsible. What's your cure for that?" Helen said.

Charles was silent. No one spoke and Helen glanced at the screen, hoping it had faded to black. No. There they were. Charles with his crutches, his bandaged head and eye, his cast. His face distorted in grief, guilt, looking at the floor. Helen sitting straight-backed in the office chair. Her expression composed, masked, immobile. Dr. Jacoby sitting opposite them in a striped French wingback chair, staring at his notepad.

"Helen. I read the report. They were hit by an unpredicted storm. Conditions deteriorated faster than they could descend. They were operating under unusually stressful conditions."

"He didn't secure the belay."

"No, no he didn't."

"If he had secured the belay, Charles Jr would be alive. He's suffering because he should suffer. No amount of counseling will change his mistake, will it, Dr. Jacoby? Will it?"

"No, Helen. I have no power in this room to change what happened."

"Helen, please," Charles' voice. Weak. Pleading. Defeated.

"I can't do this." That other Helen's voice. The next sound was the office door closing behind her.

Suddenly, another flicker and there was the hubbub of a crowd. People talking excitedly—some in English, others in Swiss. Dishes rattling. Soft music. Of course, Helen closed her eyes again. Oh yes, she thought, let's be sure to cover every one of my crimes. 1988. Lizzie's graduation dinner.

Paul's voice. "I propose a toast. To Lizzie Bancroft, who survived high school and discovered her great talent and passion for fashion design. Here's hoping you flourish in New York."

"Here, here." Glasses clinking. The sound of their small party congratulating Lizzie. Charles. Helen. Paul. Kat. That horrible man Lizzie dumped in New York, Stefan or Antoine or something. And Lizzie.

"Gifts, gifts," Kat called out. "Open ours first."

"Tell me it's not another Bible."

"Open it, silly."

The sound of wrapping paper. "Oh, a leather portfolio case! It's perfect you guys. Thanks."

"Now this one," Stefan or Antoine indicated a flat, square box. Lizzie opened it and removed a small pen and ink drawing of herself designing dresses at a drafting table while he played guitar to a large audience.

"I love it," Lizzie said, kissing the young man who looked like a greasy beatnik.

"What is it?" asked Charles.

"I could think of no finer gift for my Lizzie than to give her a vision of our beautiful future," the young man replied.

"You gave her a vision," Helen drily remarked.

"Mother, it's the best gift of all. It's perfect." Lizzie stared at her, daring her to comment further before kissing Stefan/Antoine once more to emphasize her approval of his offering. Helen rolled her eyes.

"Mine next," Charles indicating a large, lavender card.

A ripping sound. "Daddy, you're much too generous, but I'll take it! Thank you for believing in me."

"That should take a little pressure off for your first months in New York. You let me know if that runs out, but I know you'll be a hit long before."

"There's one more card," Lizzie said. "Mom, did you get me something, too?"

"She did," said Kat. "I saw her slip it in the pile earlier. You're always a surprise, Mom."

Ripping. A gasp. Then silence.

"Well, what is it, Lizzie? What did mom come up with this time?" Kat asked.

The sound of Lizzie sobbing, rushing from the table, chairs scraping, Stefan/Antoine calling after her.

Charles' bewildered tone, "Helen, what did you do?"

Kat reaching for the card then gasping, too.

"What is it, Katherine? What's in the card?"

"Two airplane tickets to Alaska and a gift card for a climbing trip for two under Lizzie's name and yours."

Helen didn't have to open her eyes to see their horrified faces looking at her again, looking at the monster who had taken up residence in the black hole that used to be Helen Bancroft.

"I won't write these things in my manuscript. I won't," she said through clenched teeth and closed eyes. But then she heard the soft whir of the Bible and she sighed. She opened her eyes and read: *Whoever conceals his transgressions will not prosper, but he who confesses and forsakes them will obtain mercy* (Proverbs 28:13).

Helen read and reread the verse, took a sip of cold coffee, picked up her pen, and wrote.

# Chapter Twelve

Helen finished the edit and checked the clock. The ink was skipping so she switched in a new cartridge. She shivered and then shuffled to the fireplace, adding two medium size logs. As she stoked the fire, she turned on public radio. A concert of Handel's Messiah.

Helen lost herself, momentarily, in the flames and in the tenor of "Comfort Ye My People" when the phone rang. Oh, Lizzie. Not again.

"Hello?"

"Gran! Gran, it's Nate."

"Nathan! It's wonderful to hear your voice! Is everything all right? Your mother isn't home from church."

"I know. I didn't want to interrupt their Christmas service by texting. I figured you wouldn't be with them."

She winced. "What's wrong?"

"It's nothing. I'm fine, Gran, fine. There's just some stuff going down here right now and I may be too busy for the next few hours to keep our Skype date tomorrow."

"I don't like the sounds of that, Nate."

"I'll be fine, Gran. No big deal. Besides, I can take care of myself. I didn't call to worry you. Just let Mom and Dad know if I don't make the family call that I'm fine. Tell them Merry Christmas and that I love them. I'll reach out when I get time."

"It's wonderful to hear your voice, young man."

"You, too, Gran. You still keeping everyone on their toes?"

"Of course. Did my package arrive?"

"Yes, and thank you, by the way. You always remember what I like."

"Peanut butter cups and steampunk novels. Those took a bit of searching to find. I had to befriend an excessively-pierced young woman in the local bookstore. She'd like to meet you when you return, by the way."

"And, as always, it was thoughtful of you to include a pre-addressed, blank thank you card."

Helen laughed. "Even a soldier should remember his manners."

A deep voice barked in the background. Helen heard scuffling and engines.

"Gran, I've got to go. I love you. You're the best, no matter what anyone else says."

"Oh, you! I love you, too, Nathan. I love you, very much. Stay safe, my boy."

"Merry Christmas! And, I will."

Helen pressed the receiver to her cheek after Nathan disconnected the call. So far from home. So near to danger.

She walked to the shelf where she kept his photo beside one of her father. Dad's face brought back the scene from the tablet of him on the floor of the barn interceding for her with God. She glanced, then, at the Bible and realized she was half-wishing it would open to some instructive passage.

As she traced Nathan's face with her finger, her knees shook. Taking a step, she dropped hard onto the overstuffed chair, unsettling Gatsby. Then, she gathered herself, looked across the room past the Bible out to the starry sky and prayed.

"I still don't believe in you, really. I realize that's not the most flattering way to start a prayer, but we're being honest tonight. I'll confess I almost want to believe right at this moment, but I've spent such a long time not believing, you know. It doesn't seem right to give up the ghost at this late hour of my life." She paused, feeling foolish for rambling and yet sensing something urging her to continue. "He's a good boy, Nathan is. Truly one of the good ones. For all that I find wrong with Katherine, she's raised her children well. I'm not sure how you like this done so I'll just get to it. Please, watch over him tonight. Keep him safe. I don't know what's happening, what danger he's in but ... well, Katherine's not like me. She couldn't bear such a loss, you know, and I wouldn't wish it on her ... on anyone."

Helen looked at her red-ink covered manuscript. "Don't do it for me. If I'm learning anything tonight, it's I've no right to ask you for anything, but Katherine's been a fan of yours since she was a girl. Surely, for her and for Paul, if you're out there, keep my grandson safe from harm. Amen."

Helen waited, listening, almost hoping to hear a still, quiet voice respond to her prayer. But, no, of course. She heard nothing. She was being silly.

She walked to the desk and looked at the title of the new chapter. "Of Toddlers and Terrorists." How apropos. The decade of grandchildren and rumblings of war.

On the day her second grandson, Harry Lee McArthur, was born, Helen emerged from the black hole. During the dark hours of the night Katherine was in labor, Helen penned the final sentence of her still unpublished novel, *My Brother, My Son.* Then, she flushed her supply of sedatives and sleeping pills prescribed by four different physicians down the toilet along with the last swallows of a tall bottle of absinthe she had purchased to better understand the minds of the great writers. She'd have fared better without that depth of understanding.

Nathan James had arrived four years earlier on a medical compound in Kijabe, Kenya. Dozens of African women had rocked that boy before he ever laid eyes on his Rhode Island Gran. Nathan was his mother's son and it was years before he warmed to Helen. His African sho-shos had darker skin and softer arms as he was wont to point out to her.

Harry, though, was another story from his very first breath drawn in the back bedroom of her home on the morning of her sixty-second birthday. Kat and Paul were on furlough stateside and, though they could avail themselves of modern conveniences, Katherine eschewed them as unnecessary and sterile. She found a local midwife named Haiti who saw them through the home birth so Harry's first cries rang out just down the hall from where Helen's first had.

Standing in the bathroom across the hall from her study, Helen heard the mewling cry. She stared long into the reflection looking back at her and faced, head-on, the monster she had become inside the black hole. Her gaze was sharp, her mouth was hard and her jaw stern and unyielding. Little lines surrounded her lips like the spikes of a dozen pitchforks and two long furrows bookended her mouth, anchoring it into a continual frown. Similar furrows seemed to be sucking her eyebrows into a facial fault line as deep as the San Andreas. Another infant cry and she imagined that tiny newborn looking up into the frightening mask she faced in the mirror. Right then, Helen resolved to push the monster down. To fight back. To change.

Charles dashed in, sleeves rolled up to his elbows, eyeglasses askew. "It's a boy, Nellie. It's a beautiful, fat, healthy boy. Come see. It's incredible."

"Charles, you've seen newborns before!" She eyed him in the mirror, marveling at the sparkle in his eyes and the lightness of his step.

"Not like this. Not one who belongs to me, to us, well, you know, not a grandchild. It's a miracle, that's what it is. What are you doing?"

"I'm fixing my make-up."

"For what?"

"For what? For the baby, that's what."

Charles took a step onto the tiled floor. "Helen, the baby doesn't care what you look like. Don't you want to see him?"

She whirled around, her face a sudden maze of tears and charcoal gray eyeliner. "Of course, of course, I want to see him but ... but ... oh, Charles."

As she dissolved into a tower of sobs and covered her face with her hands, Charles stepped near enough to put one hand on either side of her head. "Nellie. Oh, Nellie, what is it? I've never seen you like this."

"I've become a monster, Charles, a vicious, sniping, hateful monster and this baby's going to grow to hate me just as our girls have, I know it." She leaned into him and wondered how long it had been since she rested her head on his shoulder.

"Nellie, you just lost your way for a while—a long while I grant you, but I've always believed you'd find your way back to us. Harry's birth is a sign. That's what it is. Born on your birthday in the very house in which you were born, don't you see? It's a good omen for our family, Nellie, for you and me."

She looked into his eyes and sniffled as he smudged his thumbs across her cheeks. "Do you really think so, Charles?"

"I do. And if you'll dry your eyes and apply a little more of that powdery stuff there to cover the black stuff you've run over your face, you'll see for yourself."

She turned to the mirror and dabbed at her cheeks with a cloth. "Harry? Did you say his name is Harry?"

"Harry Lee. And he has ten fingers and ten toes and brown eyes and well, all the important stuff. Come on, Nellie. Come meet your birthday grandbaby."

The spare bedroom turned delivery room was beginning to lighten with the coming of morning. The lamp on the bedside table still glowed but any moment now it would be unnecessary. The room was all shades of black, white, and gray as Haiti tucked covers around Katherine and handed her a cup with a bendy straw. Katherine's usually unruly hair was smoothed back in a ponytail and headband. Her eyes were sunken and her face was puffy and pale but smiling as Helen and Charles came to the doorway.

"Mom! I'm so glad you could be here for this." Katherine's voice was hoarse and Helen could see her weariness by the way her eyelids struggled to remain even half open.

She walked over and straightened the covers, pressing the back of her hand against Kat's forehead.

Kat giggled but instead of pushing her hand away, she took it in her own and held it. "I'm not sick, Mom. This was childbirth, not chicken pox."

Helen laughed back. "Force of habit. How do you feel?"

"Amazing, actually! This was nothing like the first time. Nathan was perfectly content to remain in my womb, but this little guy was eager to breathe the fresh air of freedom." Kat handed her glass to Haiti, who was nodding.

"This was an easy delivery. You should try to take a walk around the room after a nap. I'll take the linens down to the laundry room and make you a cup of after birth tea." Haiti slipped out like an apparition and Helen looked at Kat with new admiration. How had her daughter become so strong and capable?

"Well, don't you want to see him, Mom?" Kat pointed and Helen finally noticed Paul cradling a tiny bundle in a blanket by the windows that overlooked the sea.

Paul turned to look at her. "I was just introducing him to your favorite view. Here, Helen. Come and meet the newest member of your tribe."

Her breath caught in her diaphragm and she hesitated, but Charles placed a gentle hand on the small of her back and gave her a little push.

The sun sent an exploratory ray sparkling across the waves as she drew close enough to see the tiny, bald bundle staring wide-eyed at his bearded father. "Oh, my!"

Charles stood behind her. "Didn't I tell you?"

She tried to speak, but her words caught in her throat. He was a magical baby. Alert, calm, just gazing back at Paul. She reached out and touched his tender cheek and his large brown eyes turned toward her.

"Oh, my. Hello, little man." She smiled at the sunny boy.

Charles squeezed her shoulder. "Paul, you have great circles under your eyes, son. You need a rest."

"I'm fine," said Paul.

Kat chimed in. "I agree, Paul. Come get a nap beside me."

"I really couldn't sleep, but I would like a shower. Helen, would you take him for a bit?" He pushed the little blue bundle in her direction.

"Of course, she would," Charles answered for her as he pulled the rocking chair out of the corner and into the window where the sun was promising a grand show of light even if it wouldn't be warm.

As soon as Harry was in her arms, she inhaled deeply of his newborn scent and rubbed her cheek against his head as she settled into the rocker where Momma Bea had rocked her and where her nannies had rocked her babies. She had no idea, no idea until this moment how perfectly divine it was to have no other plan than to simply cradle a child in one's arms and stare into the face of perfection.

"Mommy! Mommy!" Nathan burst into the room, his hair sticking out at all angles like a neglected paintbrush. He stopped short and his little face fell. "Hey, are you guys having a party without me? Whoa! Where did Gran get a baby?"

Everyone laughed but this only made the toddler angrier and he stamped his pajama'd foot in frustration. "What's so funny, you guys?"

Helen, in a rush of compassion, motioned for him to come near. "First, young man, it is never polite to refer to ones' elders as 'you guys.' Is that understood?"

Nathan glanced at his father before answering, "Yes, ma'am."

"Second, this wasn't a party until you arrived but now it is. In fact, it's a birthday party!"

"I love birthday parties! Is it my birthday?" Nathan asked.

"No. Today is my birthday and it's your new brother's first birthday. But you are the most honored guest because today you have become a big brother, and big brothers are the most special kind of brother there is. Would you like to see little Harry?" She lowered Harry, who was now sleeping, onto her lap and Nathan sidled up to her to look him over.

"That's Harry? How did he get out of Mommy?"

"Well, first, Mommy—" Helen started, but coughs from two nervous parents interrupted her matter-of-fact answer to a perfectly logical question. She rolled her eyes at them and modified her answer. "He came out the same way you did with a lot of encouragement from your mom and dad. What do you think of him?"

Nathan looked him over as everyone else watched. He inched closer to Helen as he did and placed a chubby hand on her arm. The tenderness of it brought tears to her eyes. "Does he do anything except sleep?"

Charles chuckled, but she shushed him with a glance. "Not too much just yet. It's very tiring to have a first birthday so you'll have to do most of the celebrating and you'll have to eat most of the cake."

"Cake! We're having cake! For breakfast?"

"No, but later we'll have cake and perhaps I can rustle up some balloons for the occasion. Would you like that?"

Nathan nodded and then turned to his parents with a stage whisper. "Hey, I thought you said Gran isn't fun. She sounds fun to me!"

The adults all held their breath, but Helen startled the baby and had to settle him back on her shoulder as she laughed so hard she must have laughed away a million of those face lines.

Helen finished reading this section and realized she felt no need to apply her red pen, but the pages of the Bible turned. "No. No. What could you possibly have to say about this?" she said as she pulled the book toward her and read with relief and amazement, *Above all, love each other deeply, because love covers over a multitude of sins* (I Peter 4:8).

Why this made her cry more than any other verse tonight, she didn't know, but for several long moments, Helen wept.

# Chapter Thirteen

Sitting with Charles in an overly verdant garden on the grounds of the hospital in Kenya where Paul served as medical director, Helen sipped her iced tea and shared a thought.

"I'm concerned about the future, Charles."

"Future?" he replied. "We're more than set for the coming years, Nellie. Where is this coming from?" He pointed and she nodded as she spied the family of giraffes he was watching across the plain.

"Grandchildren. My grandchildren and their future. I'm worried about the world we're leaving them. That's where this is coming from, Charles. We have to do more."

Grandchildren had sent the monster Helen deep into hiding, but there were other monsters at large in this decade. In the February after Harry was born, a terrorist group bombed the World Trade Center. The damage wasn't as horrendous as they'd planned, but the act of violence on American soil planted a seed of anxiety and familial unrest in Helen's mind. She took her role as matriarch seriously. The first thing she did was set up generous trusts for Nate and Harry, but she longed to impact their futures in more global ways.

The feeling was reinforced in April 1995 when her third grandchild, Madison, was born in Kenya. That same month, Timothy McVeigh bombed a federal building in Oklahoma City. The photo of a firefighter cradling a tiny victim, little one-year-old Baylee Almon, moved Helen to purchase seats for them on a flight to Kenya the next month so they could hold the newest member of the family.

Charles popped a fig into his mouth. "What, exactly, do you propose we do?"

"I've spoken with Paul. I'd like to raise funds for a girls' school here in Kijabe like the one I helped to found in Afghanistan."

"And how do you plan to fit that in with your work for the Feminist Majority Foundation, editing, and writing, may I ask?" Charles lowered the brim of his hat over his eyes.

"I'll make it work. I'm an amazing woman."

"Well, you amaze me."

She hadn't expected her charity to completely heal her relationship with Kat, but she never imagined it be a setback. The two of them had a whispering argument that night as she rocked six-week-old Maddie. Kat paced the oil lamp-lit nursery.

"I thought you'd be happy. I want to support your work. I have much to make up for in life, you agree with that. This is a start," Helen whispered, thinking she was displaying admirable humility.

Kat wet a cloth in the basin and used it to cool the back of her neck and her arms. Helen admired Kat's slender, muscular frame, recovered quickly even after her third child. Life in Kenya suited her. She was strong here, lovely, and purposeful. Helen envied her here.

Kat turned to her with her worried face. "It's just, I feel as though you're still not understanding what we do here is all about. It's not about being good, it's about representing Jesus."

Nellie held Maddie up to her shoulder and rapped firmly on her little back. "Christians haven't cornered the market on goodness, Kat. The school I've helped support in Afghanistan is a good thing and I did it on my own, without a nudge from the Almighty. I just want to do that here. Paul liked the idea. Why don't you?"

"See, that's exactly what I mean. You take total credit." Kat replied.

"Why shouldn't I take credit? It's my work. What exactly is Jesus against? Good work or me getting the credit?"

Kat sighed. "He's not against it, that's not what I'm saying at all. It's a good idea. It's a great idea. My problem is with you thinking you can buy your way into God's good graces by doing it." She wrapped her arms around her waist and leaned against the crib.

"You're wrong on all counts. I have no interest in being in God's good graces. I believe more in karma than I do in the bully God you seem so fond of who wants everything His own way. This school is good karma. You're the first Christian I've ever known to be bothered by someone wanting to do good. You'd definitely be the first one to turn down a donation." Helen could hear the monster growl somewhere deep in her mind.

"You're not hearing me, Mom. I'm thrilled you've taken an interest in our work. But there isn't enough good karma in the universe to make yourself good."

"You really think I'm that bad."

"I think we all are. I don't want you to think this act of good will save your soul."

"Or win me any traction with you."

"You don't need traction with me. I love you, Mom."

"You've a funny way of showing it."

"No, Mom. I just have the same issue with you that God does, I suppose. Jesus doesn't want your money or your good works or your accomplishments, He just wants you."

"You have me. I've flown halfway around the world for you. To spend time with you. Isn't that good enough?"

"Of course, it's good enough, Mom. I love that you're here. I love that you spend time with the boys."

"But, I'll never be truly good enough for you unless I accept Jesus, too."

"I will never stop wanting you to accept Jesus, no, but that doesn't mean you're not good enough for me."

"It certainly sounds like it and feels like it." Maddie started to wail and Helen realized she'd been pounding harder and harder on the poor little one's back trying to produce a burp and process her frustration with Kat at the same time.

"Here. Let me." Kat reached for her.

"Fine. I'm tired out anyway." Helen bolted from the chair and left the room, ignoring Kat's pleas to remain.

The next morning, a warm, rainy Sunday, they attended worship service at the simple chapel with the family out of respect for Paul and Kat. Helen enjoyed the children's singing, the drums, and the congregational music accompanied by the driving rain. It beat hard on the wooden roof and overhang but the worshipers remained dry despite that the structure had no walls. Their intimacy was accentuated by the show of nature around them—lightning striking miles out on the plain.

Helen was flanked by Charles on one side and little Harry on the other. She was proud he wasn't a fidgety child and, even at two-and-one-half, seemingly enrapt by the morning's speaker. When she turned to whisper so to Charles, she was startled to find Charles similarly mesmerized. Helen scowled but refocused on the preacher trying to hear what they heard. Instead, the minister's words bounced off her mind like the rain on the roof and she withdrew into a sense she was missing something everyone else saw.

Distracted, she nearly missed the cue to stand for prayer. The sincere, bespectacled young Kenyan preacher paused before pronouncing the benediction to ask if anyone had been moved by the teaching to repent of their sins and accept Jesus Christ as the Savior of their souls. Helen stared down at her feet, expecting the congregation to cough politely as they did at her childhood Presbyterian Church before the preacher moved on but instead, she felt the soft movement of people leaving their seats and walking forward to kneel, weep, and pray at the rough-hewn altar.

Suddenly, she realized the seats on either side of her were vacant. At the altar, side-by-side, were Charles and little Harry. Charles' face was awash with tears. Little Harry was composed but earnest, his little hands together and his head bowed.

Helen leaned over and touched her hand to Kat's arm. "What's happening?" she asked.

Kat shook her head. "I've never seen anything like this here. Do you see Dad and Harry? Oh, Mom, isn't it beautiful?" Tears streamed down Kat's face, but Helen fought a rising panic.

What had they heard that she hadn't? Why was she being left out of this moment, closed off from some divine insight that could be heard by old men and children but not by her? She felt nothing. She'd listened, but the preacher's words hadn't moved her. All she felt as she stared at her husband, now on his knees surrounded by several men, their hands on his head praying and crying out, was embarrassment, fear, and loneliness. A loneliness like no other she'd ever known. As if this moment had ripped from her whatever intimacy with her family she'd built in these years since Harry's birth. She just wanted to go home.

Charles bent down and scooped Harry into his arms. When Harry wrapped his little arms around his granddad's neck and kissed him on the cheek, the congregation clapped and cheered. Helen couldn't take any more. She snatched her umbrella and dashed out alone into the driving rain.

Helen was sad all over again reading her memory of the day of Charles' conversion and she felt the lateness of the hour. Perhaps that's why she hadn't heard the turning pages of the Bible but the glow of a new verse caught her eye. *For the message of the cross is foolishness to those who are perishing, but to us who are being saved it is the power of God. For it is written: "I will destroy the wisdom of the wise; the intelligence of the intelligent I will frustrate"* (I Corinthians 1:18-19).

"That is precisely what I felt that morning—destroyed and frustrated," Helen said. She kept reading further in that passage, fascinated by the words of the Biblical writer that seemed to be describing her experience of the gospel.

When she was done, she looked out at the sea. "Am I perishing?" she asked aloud. Then the words of the old Navy hymn came back to her and she sang them softly, "O hear us when we cry to Thee, For those in Peril on the sea."

"Don't you love Jesus, too, Gran?" Harry's four-year-old voice came from the tablet and she looked over to a scene she'd forgotten completely. It was late afternoon on the day of Caroline's birth, here in the same room where Harry had entered the world and everyone else was napping. Just before Kat went into labor, she and Helen had exchanged cross words so Helen was brooding on the porch in a great rattan chair, watching the rain as it danced on the ocean waves. Little Harry had been napping in a papa-san chair nearby but woke up at a burst of thunder, clambering into her lap. Now, she realized, he'd overheard the two women he loved as they fought earlier.

"Don't you, Gran? Love Jesus?" Harry repeated.

"It's impolite to ask people about religion, Harry," she tried.

"What's 'ligion, Gran?"

"Re-ligion is talking about God," she replied.

"Oh, well. Our family is impolite all the time. I think there's different rules about impolite in Africa than in America." He yawned.

"That's probably true." She stroked his hair, so like Charles.

"But, Jesus isn't 'ligion, Gran. Jesus is Jesus. He loves everyone. Mom and Daddy love Jesus. Nate loves Jesus. Me and Grandpa—"

"Grandpa and I," she corrected.

"Grandpa and I love Jesus. I 'spect Maddie and Cara will love him soon, too. It's very, very important to love Jesus. You know that, don't you?" Harry put a chubby hand on either side of her face and pressed his nose to her nose. "You must love Jesus, Gran," he said in a goofy little voice that made her laugh.

"Maybe someday I will. I don't know him very well right now," she said, hoping to end the conversation.

"Oh, it's easy to know him. There's stories about him. Lots of stories. I know some of them. Do you want me to tell you one?"

"I think I would rather read a story to you. Why don't you run over to those shelves and grab the old green one with the elephant on the cover and I will read to you about the great, grey-green, greasy Limpopo River."

"Yea!"

Harry was easily distracted from his evangelistic tactics at four, but he never lost his passion for them and it wasn't his last attempt to get through to her.

# Chapter Fourteen

The nineties passed with trips by both families across the sea that rolled between them. Kat and Paul resided in Kenya with a furlough year in Newport every four. Helen and Charles visited them in-between. Lizzie traveled from one misadventure to another, only calling home to request advances on her inheritance.

The nineties were also the decade of Charles' transformation. He immersed himself in Bible study and regular meetings with a local pastor who took to tutoring him in all things Christian. He thrived. Helen allowing her isolation to drive her to greater deeds of charity and to doting on grandchildren, reserving their future respect if not their mother's, hoping charity would fill the growing divide between herself and Charles.

Now, Helen edited freely the sections that were clearly unworthy. She enjoyed staying ahead of the flipping Bible. She drew red through her underhanded dealings with her siblings as she'd secured the family home for herself. She'd originally included the story because she'd thought herself practical and clever, making a move to protect the inheritance for her grandchildren. Somehow, now she saw it as the selfish theft it was.

She red-penned the cruel fights with Lizzie, her criticism of Kat, the mocking commentary she maintained at every phase of Charles' conversion. Initially, she'd admired her feisty nature, envisioned herself something of a character in a series on public television—the witty older woman everyone secretly admires. But now, her words just read as unloving, self-serving, and mean.

Charles tried, often, to reason her into conversion. Two years after Cara's birth, they'd spent Christmas in Kenya, even purchasing a ticket for Lizzie to join them. Christmas night, Kat and Charles double-teamed her over coffee. The children slept worn out from a day of gifts and fun. The adults sat around the kitchen table picking at leftover dessert and nuts.

Charles started the intervention. "Did you know the book I gave you this morning on Christianity was written by a journalist, Nellie? His wife became a Christian and he set out to debunk the faith for her. Ended up believing it himself."

"You should like that book, Mom," Kat said.

Lizzie sneered. "Why would Mom like any book about Jesus? Just because a reporter wrote it? That's pretty shallow thinking. You two are grasping at straws."

"You might like it, too, Lizzie," Charles said softly.

Lizzie snorted. "Why? Couldn't you find a book written by a Christian who failed at fashion design?"

"Why is everything a joke to you?" Kat stood, clearing dishes into the sink.

"Why do you keep picking at Mom about religion? You've got Dad on board your little ark, leave Mom alone." Lizzie sliced a large piece of squash pie and thunked it onto her plate, then covered it and most of the dish with whipped cream.

"Leave your sister alone, Elizabeth. I'm the one who bought the book and I'm the one who brought it up." Charles said.

"Well, great, then you're the one who should drop it." Lizzie stuck her tongue out at Charles then took a large bite of pie, chomping and smacking loudly.

Paul chimed in. "Lizzie, I know your sister and Dad only bring this up out of love for your mom—and for you. This writer presents a rational case for the truth of Jesus Christ. Your dad respects your mom's intelligence and has found something that would address her questions about Christianity."

"What makes any of you think Mom has questions about Christianity?" Lizzie licked her spoon and turned to Helen. "Mom? Do you have questions about Christianity?"

Helen's face burned and she looked up from the table center, which had been her focus since the start of the conversation. "I do, actually. My one question, in fact, is why any of you think I would ever consider following a religion that says my son and my brother are already condemned to hell." Her voice caught and the sob in her throat shocked her more than anyone, as she turned on Charles. "You, of all of them, should know I could never imagine wanting to go someplace that AJ and Charles Jr are not wanted. I much prefer to believe that one day I will join them both in the warm earth and that will be the end of it."

Charles' face had softened, grown wiser and more handsome these past years. His eyes glistened now, as he replied, "But what if it's not the end, Nellie? How can you imagine I wouldn't try everything in my power to spend eternity with you?"

Lizzie cursed as her pie plate crashed onto the table. They turned to find her shaking, twitching, and jerking her arms and head.

Helen stood. "Charles? Paul?"

Paul's and Charles' chairs scraped the floor as they stood. Paul put one hand on either side of Lizzie's face. "Lizzie. What did you take?"

Lizzie's head bounced around in Paul's hand and her teeth chattered.

"Lizzie!" Paul barked. "Answer me."

"D—don't flip out. A prescription my friend said would c-c-calm me down on the visit. And my re-regular stuff. Took a little extra of both."

Charles rushed to her purse and pulled out two bottles. "Hers is Citalopram. This other one is Tramadol."

Paul remained calm. "Fantastic."

"I'm s-s-sorry. I-I-I just w-w-wanted to b-b-b n-normal f-f-f-or the visit." She slumped and the twitching increased.

"Well, you're normal for this family," Paul replied as he scooped Lizzie into his arms.

"She'll be fine," Charles said confidently as the two carried her out to the clinic leaving Kat and Helen staring after them.

Kat spoke first. "Is she ever going to pull herself together?"

"Oh, and you're so perfect?" Helen cleared dishes into the sink.

"No. What? Seriously, you're going to defend this?" Kat started slamming items into the refrigerator.

"She's having a seizure, not robbing a bank." Helen yanked at the water knobs and swung the faucet over the dirty dishes.

A crashing sound made her turn to face Kat, standing over a puddle of coffee and shattered carafe. "I give up, Mom. I absolutely give up. I don't know what exactly I would have to do to win your approval, but apparently it involves substance abuse and screwing up my life. Those seem to be the only activities sure to bring out your maternal instincts."

Kat snatched a sweater from a hook and ran from the house, the screen door smacking the doorframe behind her. Helen completed the cleanup alone.

Helen looked up at the bookcase on the north wall. Did she still have the book Charles gave her that Christmas? She'd never read it, but she'd saved it. She saved every book.

There. She spied it on the highest shelf and pulled her step stool over. She took it to her overstuffed chair and opened the front cover. *"To my Nellie, Because of the truth illustrated in this book, I can now honestly promise to love you forever. Your Charles."* After allowing herself a moment with the familiar ache of missing him like a lost limb, Helen turned to the first page and began to read.

# Chapter Fifteen

The clock chimed. Nine p.m. Helen looked up. The book had absorbed her attention for forty-five minutes. Well-written. No sentimentality. She wished Charles was beside her so she could ask his forgiveness for receiving it with little grace. He was right, of course. It was the perfect book for her to read on the subject. It scratched the itch that this evening had created like a heat rash in her mind. How dearly she missed having someone close who knew her well.

She wanted to read on, but her own story rested unfinished on the desk.

She glanced at the coffee pot but passed. No sound downstairs. Helen tuned her ear to the radio news and focused on the photos of Charles and Nathan as she absorbed one headline that caught her attention.

"A Christmas Eve raid of an American military outpost in Afghanistan has resulted in American casualties. Details still emerging. We'll keep you informed as this story develops."

Ice. There was no other metaphor for this feeling she'd experienced too many times in years past. Ice in her veins. Sheer dread.

Images of Nathan under fire. Young men and women falling to the ground or flying through the air. Terrible images. Falling.

Helen snatched her cane and tossed the book onto the floor. There was nothing she could do. Nothing. She was just an old woman in a room with no power to protect her grandson from enemy fire or her daughter from the loss of a child.

But, no. If God existed, he wouldn't do this. He wouldn't take their child. He would have heard their prayers, Paul's and Kat's, if not hers. If she didn't have her own faith, she would rest on theirs for now.

Nothing to do but keep editing. Think about something else. Anything. Not Afghanistan. Not soldiers in harm's way. Not AJ. Not Charles Jr. Just focus and complete the dare. Save Harry. Finish out this decade. The decade defined by the terrible, terrible event that changed everything.

She grabbed her pen and turned the page.

September 11, 2001.

She was home alone with the four grandchildren. At twelve, eight, six, and four, they were a handful but manageable. Everyone was out except the staff. Charles was volunteering at the homeless shelter. Paul and Kat had left Sunday night for a four-day missionary conference in Illinois. Breakfast was over and she'd allowed the children to watch a video while she sipped her coffee and read the paper. As the video ended, Nathan kept the television on, flipping through the channels.

Helen didn't glance up before instructing him. "Nathan, I said one video and then you older three need to get going on the school assignments your mother left you."

"Just a second, Gran," he replied.

She looked up over her reading glasses. "Now."

Harry pointed at the screen. "Hey, we went there, didn't we, Gran? To visit Aunt Lizzie. I remember those tall buildings. One's on fire!"

Helen looked at the screen. Black smoke billowing from one of the twin towers. The anchor saying something about a plane. A terrible accident. They had an eyewitness on the phone saying it was a large plane; a passenger jet, perhaps. The anchor questioning the validity of that information. Could they have seen a small plane? Maybe not a jet?

Nathan turned to her, eyes wide. "Gran? Is this real?"

The children's American nanny, Erin, appeared at the door. "Ma'am, something's happened in New York."

"Yes, Erin. I'm watching it." Helen's eyes were on the screen, trying to read the ticker, listen, and think at the same time. "Please, take the girls into the playroom, would you? Girls, go with Erin." Helen kept her voice level, but it was an effort. The news footage brought back memories of the bombing in the early nineties, but this wasn't a bomb. *Just a terrible accident, still—*

"Oh, wow! Gran! Was that another plane? Did that plane just fly into the other tower?" Nathan pointed at the TV with the remote still in his hand. Harry scrambled to stand beside her chair. She leaned forward trying to hear the news anchor who was grasping for explanations herself.

An air traffic control problem? Couldn't be an accident now. Not two planes. The anchors fumbling to narrate and offer facts they didn't yet have. Their voices rising. Phones in the background. Helen flashing back to the Hindenburg, the announcer's screams, AJ's tears, her father's face.

"Gran?" Harry tugged at her sleeve. "Are there people in those buildings? In the planes?"

More footage. Different angles. Yes, it was a second plane. Yes, it struck the second tower. Replay. Yes, it was a passenger jet. Nate stared at her, his face twisted with questions and astonishment. What's happening? Harry inched closer.

The phone rang.

Charles. "Something's happening."

"I know. We're watching it."

"Who?"

"The boys are with me. Erin took the girls to the nursery."

"Harry?"

"I know. But he's seen it already."

"I'm almost there."

A third plane flew into the Pentagon. A fourth was rumored heading for the White House. Smoke billowing from the towers. All planes in American airspace grounded.

Harry climbed into her lap and Nathan sat cross-legged on the floor beside her chair. "Gran, what's happening? Are they going to kill the president? We just learned about his dog, Barney. Are they going to kill Barney?"

"No one is going to kill the president or Barney." Helen closed her eyes for a moment seeing grainy black-and-white news footage of a motorcade in Dallas.

"What's happening then? How far is Illinois from the fourth plane?" Nathan persisted.

"I'm not sure what's happening, Nathan, but we're safe here and your parents are nowhere near New York."

"Aunt Lizzie?"

Lizzie.

Helen dialed her home phone and left a voice mail. Dialed her cell. The mailbox was full. Helen steadied herself with facts. Lizzie had no business at the trade centers. She would have been at work before the first plane hit. Evacuated, maybe. Safe, certainly.

Harry watched the TV mesmerized, chewing his bottom lip. He spoke in a small voice, almost a whisper. "Will they get the people out, Gran? I don't see any firefighters. Aren't they going to put out the fire?"

"Firefighters? I'm sure they're there, Harry. Don't chew your lip. This camera angle is high up. We 're seeing the buildings from the sky." She took the remote from Nathan and switched through the news networks. "There. See. The ground cameras are showing fire trucks and police and firefighters."

"They'll rescue the people inside the buildings?" Harry asked, pressing himself into Helen.

Charles walked into the room and laid a hand on Harry's head as he stared at the screen. "Of course, my boy. Of course. People who live in big cities practice things like this. I'm sure the people in the buildings are evacuating now and firefighters are helping them."

Nathan jumped up. "One of the buildings fell down!"

"What? No, impossible," Charles said, taking the remote from Helen and increasing the volume. "There, the announcer said something fell off the building. Listen."

*We have one of our crew on the ground on the phone. Can you tell us what happened? It looked like something fell off the South Tower.*

*It collapsed. The South Tower collapsed onto itself like a demolition. It's terrible.*

*A wall of the tower collapsed?*

*The entire building collapsed. It's not there anymore!*

Helen and Charles stared, speechless. Harry hid his face. Nathan dashed to the phone. "I'm calling my dad."

Harry burrowed his head into Helen's sweater. "They can't save the people inside now."

Recorded here—her memories of that day and the ones that followed. Some were sharp with solid borders like the first hour alone with the boys. Others melded into one long, hazy montage of news broadcasts and phone calls. For days, they were glued to either the television or the phone, their lifeline to loved ones.

Paul and Kat were overwrought. Grounded so far from the children. Frantic to be home, guiding them through this nightmare, coaching Helen on what to say and how to explain it. Lamenting the timing of their furlough, the conference. Second-guessing their decision to take an assignment stateside. Then, grief-stricken at the news that Paul's best friend, a firefighter, was inside the South Tower when it collapsed. The pair finally rented a car, driving straight through to be home.

And Lizzie. Their New Yorker. Lizzie lost so many and so much. Her city life intersected with those who had died or who lost someone in more ways than she could explain through the hours of calls home. There were days of terror in the Big Apple. Charles wanted her back in Rhode Island but how could she leave? This was her city. This was her home. She had stood out in the street as it happened and looked up, her lungs filling with ashes and dust, watching bodies fall from the sky onto unforgiving pavement. If she had ever had a hope of emotional stability, it collapsed that day into the rubble of Ground Zero.

Later in the afternoon of the first day, Helen checked on her sisters. Mary had died two years earlier following a stroke, Gladys a month later of pancreatic cancer, and Maudie was in a facility for Alzheimer's patients so Helen called their children. Touched base. Consoled. Counted heads.

She reached Molls, who lived in Virginia now. Several of her children were career military, but none were in the Pentagon that Tuesday morning. Dodie took days to reach but only because she and her husband had been on an unexpectedly extended vacation in Europe when air traffic to the US halted. They were shaken but whole.

Tucking the boys into bed that first night, Harry grabbed her hand. She sat on the covers and inspected his fingernails. "What is it, Harry? You need a good scrubbing tomorrow."

"Where is Grandpa? Can he tuck me in?"

"Grandpa's talking with Aunt Lizzie. I'll send him to check on you when he's through. Everything is fine, Harry. We're all safe and your parents are safe, too."

"Will you say a prayer with me, Gran?" his brown eyes, so deep like vats of chocolate, made her wish that she believed. She wished, for Harry's sake, that she believed like she wished there was truly a Santa Claus and gold at the end of the rainbow.

"Why don't you pray and I'll listen," she said. "Would that be all right?"

He nodded as he folded his hands. "Dear Jesus, please keep us all safe from the bad men who flew planes into the towers and the Pentagon today and the one that crashed in the field. Watch over Mom and Dad and Aunt Lizzie too. Jesus, I'm sad for all the people who died today, especially the ones who are still out there in the dark. If any of them have little kids, I hope you'll take special care of them tonight so they aren't so sad their hearts break. But if they do break, Jesus, I pray you put them back together. Thank you that we were with Gran today when this bad thing happened. She's good at explaining things even if she doesn't love you yet. Please forgive Gran and please forgive the bad men who flew all those planes. Amen."

When he finished, he leaned up and kissed her cheek. She held his shoulders, lingering near the warmth of his sweaty forehead, inhaling the innocence of him.

As he settled down and closed his eyes, she watched him. She tried to remember having that faith as a child. Something had softened in her as his little voice prayed but then she remembered another child, one with braids praying for a brother's safety and the memory was a puff of air, extinguishing the flicker of light in her heart.

Then, she thought about the last line of his prayer, "Please forgive Gran and please forgive the bad men who flew all those planes." What crazy religion would lump her in the same lot as murdering terrorists? They were misguided religious zealots, probably thought they were serving their own god and that was certainly a lie. How was Harry ever going to sort through this complex world he was sure to inherit? How could she distinguish herself to him from extremists who fly planes into buildings?

She vowed to be there for him when his own faith came crashing down around his dreams. She did not know a God who saves. She knew a world where towers collapsed, planes crashed, and evil won the day. One day, Harry would know that world, too, and then he would need her.

# Chapter Sixteen

"The Fruit of Many Labors"

What else would one call this past decade? The season of summation. Years of accolades and awards. Retirement and reinvention. Charles' last days.

The decade began with a lavish wedding. 9/11 jumpstarted many stalled lives, Lizzie's among them. In June of 2002, she catapulted into marriage with Gavin Caulfield, an unassuming, milquetoast schoolteacher. She dazzled him long enough for a walk down a very expensive aisle for which Helen coughed up a sizable donation to the First Presbyterian Church of Newport. Lizzie felt a connection there because her grandfather had attended, but Helen hadn't darkened the doors enough times to merit an easy reservation for their preferred wedding day.

Helen stood with Kat in the churchyard watching Lizzie, a bride lost in frothy mounds of white taffeta like a meringue before being baked, greet three hundred guests as they filed from the stone church.

"I wouldn't have figured Lizzie for the all the pomp and circumstance, would you?" Kat observed.

Helen held up one hand. "I have never been able to predict that girl. Tradition all the way. She's baffled me from the department store registry for china right down to the candied almond favors. The only thing I can reliably predict with Lizzie is that it'll require large amounts of cash."

Kat laughed. "Well, maybe this is the turning point. Marriage and children will finally settle her down."

"I give it eighteen months,"

It took nine years, but Lizzie managed to screw up not only her marriage, but also her three lovely brown-eyed babies—Milo, Benson, and Poppy. She also succeeded in convincing Gavin that Helen was toxic so the extent of her relationship with those three grandchildren was restricted to gifts at holidays, school photos, and the occasional awkward phone conversation when Gavin needed an update on Lizzie's latest Western Union address.

Three funerals followed the wedding. Helen's friend and editor, Jim Daniels. His big heart finally gave out. Molls and her husband were memorialized together a week after their car was struck by a drunk driver. Then, on a sunny August day beneath the bluest sky, she stood with Charles and a dismal knot of mourners on a hill overlooking the ocean to say farewell to Montgomery Salinger.

They'd learned of his death in the paper and were surprised that only a graveside service was planned. Once the cars had parked and twelve people created a ragged semi-circle around the gravesite, a young man who had been speaking with the funeral director turned to address the group. Helen gasped. It was the same face that had captured her heart across a ballroom when she was a girl. She teetered and Charles strengthened his grasp around her waist.

"Thank you all for coming." Monty's young twin began. "My great-grandfather was a complicated man. He lived long enough to soften around the edges and forge a fragile peace with the demons he brought home from war. For some men, that will have to be enough.

I pray it was enough for him." He pulled from behind the coffin a shot glass and bottle of Crown Royal whiskey, pouring a double shot before he continued.

Raising the glass, he said, "He loved Newport. He loved whiskey. I'll say this for him, he never forgot his friends who didn't make it home from war. Here's to you, Pops. May God grant you peace and a spot at the bar." He drained the shot and set the glass, upside down, on the coffin.

That was all.

He shook each mourner's hand, smiling politely when he reached Helen and Charles. "Thank you for coming. I'm Harlan. I'm sorry that I don't know you."

Charles gripped the boy's hand. "We were friends of your grandfather's from just after the war. Charles and Helen Bancroft."

Harlan looked at her sharply. "Helen?"

She smiled, still unable to get over the likeness. "Your grandfather used to call me Nellie."

Harlan nodded. "He spoke of you often. My grandmother left years ago. She started over in Arizona. There were many women in his life after her." He shrugged. "None stayed. I lived with him this last year. He was tough. Drove everyone else away but he talked all the time about his war buddies and the only girl he ever loved. You."

Helen felt like a schoolgirl. "That's very kind of you to say, Harlan."

"Not kindness, the truth. If you don't mind me saying, I see why you lingered in Pop's mind through the years." He winked at Charles. "You're a lucky man, Mr. Bancroft."

He went on to greet the last mourner. Helen stared at the shot glass-adorned casket, finding it hard to see clearly, the bonny day suddenly misty. Charles stood behind her and she leaned into him for a long time.

Helen paused before turning the page. Would the tablet call her on her lie?

Of course. The Bible's pages turned to Luke 8:17: *For there is nothing hidden that will not be disclosed, and nothing concealed that will not be known or brought out into the open* ... even as the gadget sprang into action.

There they were. She and Charles holding one another, taking in Monty's casket under the August sky as the other mourners departed. She dabbed at her eyes as Charles turned her around to face him.

"Do you have regrets, Nellie?"

"Everyone has regrets, Charles. Don't you?"

"That's not what I mean and you know it. Harlan said you were the love of Monty's life. Was he the love of yours? Do you regret that you ended up with me instead of him?"

She paused as her bottom lip trembled.

She moistened her lips and looked at the ground before looking up again.

She hesitated a moment more.

His shoulders slumped and he stared away. "I'm sorry, Nellie. I know I wasn't your first choice. I've disappointed you. You're the love of my life, though, even if I'm not the love of yours."

"Charles—"

"No," He placed a finger to her lips. "You would never say such a cruel thing aloud. Your silence speaks the truth." He looked at the coffin. "Take a moment to say good-bye." He turned and walked to the car.

Helen stood alone beside the gleaming casket. She had no words for this wooden shroud nor for the stranger housed within. Charles was the love of her life, but she had paused; she had paused knowing it would hurt him—wanting still to hurt him. She needed to hurt him for Jean, for Charles Jr, for Jesus, for the hundreds of ways he was more whole than she was and for the pure love he offered despite her serrated edges.

But the dagger she jabbed into his chest pierced her heart as well. The monster Helen still lurked; perhaps she was more monster than woman now. Maybe she still wondered about Monty because he was the man she'd deserved, not Charles.

The screen faded with her still standing beside the casket in the sun.

A thousand little cruelties she'd dispensed, most often to those she'd been entrusted to love. The weight of them now, like single snowflakes collecting to collapse a rooftop, pressed in on her.

There were reasons—anger, spite, revenge, control—always reasons, but in the glow of the Bible verses and the mysterious tablet, it just felt like ugly, self-serving malevolence. Guilt bore down on her like unrelenting winds straining the sails of a ship in a storm and she felt that to snap would be relief.

She didn't like this. Her skin crawled. She wanted to break things. To weep. To walk onto the beach and scream at the surf and sky. This was her life. The life she'd built. A life she'd been proud to write. Her heritage to her grandchildren and now … now some twist of perception was distorting it—like the bad trips those pimply teenagers took at Woodstock. Where would it lead?

She read the rest. The grand celebration of her 75th birthday. Another one for Charles' 80th. They were well-attended, both. People honored them—lauded and praised their lives of good works and respectability. They were good people. Others agreed.

Still, she remembered the speech Charles made at his party. She'd recorded it here because those in attendance thought it beautiful. It had always haunted her.

"Thank you all, not only for coming tonight but for every way in which you've touched my life over the years. I count myself as deeply blessed and you all are the reason."

Charles stopped to compose himself before continuing. "A few years back, I would have declared my life a good one. I'm not a perfect man, but I've worked hard and loved well. Once, I thought that was enough. But one Sunday morning in Africa, I came to see my life through the eyes of a loving God and I found it lacking."

He took a sip of water and continued. "Not in good works. I had those. Not in human love. I have been blessed with that. Not even in awe and miracles. As a man of medicine, I've witnessed my share of miracles and even pulled off a couple."

This brought a polite ripple of laughter.

"No, on that morning in Africa, I saw for the first time that even with all that was good, I was missing what was best. That though I have saved the lives of others, I could not manufacture my own salvation. That standing before a perfect God who offered me forgiveness, freedom, love, and salvation, I was a wretch worthy of hell for turning my back on His outstretched hands for most of my life." His voice caught in a sob and fat tears rolled down his cheeks. "To think I almost missed it, the best that life has to offer, a relationship with Jesus Christ."

The guests were silent. Nellie had so looked forward to his speech, expecting to be the recipient of his gratitude, the star of his life story. She knew he was religious now, but this was beyond humiliating. This personal emotional speech in front of everyone. Kat's eyes brimmed with pride, but Lizzie rolled hers, strumming her fingers on the table linen. Nellie stared at her hands clenched in her lap as he continued.

"Friends, I ask your forgiveness and the forgiveness of those closest to me, especially my children and my dear Nellie. What a better life I could have offered you, what a better husband, father, healer, and friend I could have been if I had chosen to give you more than just myself but also the love of Christ. This is what I offer you now and will offer you for the days that remain until I see Him face to face. You honor the man

I was and for that, I thank you. But please, know that man died when I knelt before an altar on a sunny day in Kenya and stood up a new man. A man saved and redeemed by the power of the Almighty God, Jesus Christ. I lived all the years before for myself. The days that remain, I live for him. Thank you."

There was an awkward silence as he returned to his seat. Coughing. A chair scrape. Then polite, brief applause that only had to last until Paul arrived at the microphone to announce the band was open for requests.

She knew it hurt him that she stared at her lap, even after he returned to the table. She knew he wished for her to kiss his cheek, pat his hand, and assure him his speech was lovely but she hadn't. She hadn't said anything cruel. She let her silence slip the dagger beneath his unguarded ribcage.

Then one snowy morning, three short years later, she awoke with him cold beside her. There was never a moment before or since when she had been more alone than that moment. He'd slipped from her sometime in the night without so much as a kiss goodbye. If he and Kat were right, he was enjoying heaven already while she was left with the mess of their lives here on earth.

"Why?" she asked aloud, staring at the Bible. "Why are you turning everything upside down? Life was good. I was good. It was all good until tonight!"

The pages of the Bible turned to Psalm 106:1, *Praise the Lord. Give thanks to the Lord, for he is good; his love endures forever.*

"Is that what this is about? I not only need to believe you exist, but I'm supposed to thank you, too? Believe in your goodness? No. I can't explain this, all that has happened tonight but no, I won't say that you're good! If you were good, AJ wouldn't have died. If you were good, Charles Jr would still be alive. If you were good, you wouldn't have taken the best of Charles from me in our final years! If you were good, my grandson would be safe here, enjoying Christmas with his family, not fighting for his life in some desert caves half a world away. No! No, sir. You are not good!"

She slammed her hand down and a blast of red ink squirted from the pen onto the final page of her manuscript blotting the remainder of the chapter in crimson.

"Look at what you've done," she said as she pulled at the pages. "This was my gift for Harry. This was the record of my life—my best memories, my greatest accomplishments but now look at it. Marked up and torn apart by your Book and your select memories of my worst moments."

She shuffled the pages and saw edit after edit. She searched for enough work that wasn't marked with red so she could make her case. And then she realized the horrible truth.

"There isn't enough. This won't do it. This won't convince Harry. There are more red pen edits than there is life that survived the dare. Now you've undone me completely." Helen stared at the Bible as though it was a person. For a long moment, she considered in silence what she had just done to her own life story.

Then, she spoke quietly to the Bible but the rage behind her words left her nearly breathless. "My life has been built on words. A woman of words. A crafter of words. My life was full of words and I used beautiful, perfect words to record it here but now … now … what has become of my love of words? Because of you, my own words have betrayed me and I have nowhere left to turn."

She swept the manuscript off her desk and the pages flew around the study like eight and a half-by-eleven-inch snowflakes spattered with red—with stain—with blood.

Helen squeezed her eyelids tight trying to control her emotions, regain her composure, look out at the darkened sea, and find her way to a calm shore within herself, but the Bible flipped its pages one last time and she knew she shouldn't but she forced herself to look.

John 1:1— *In the beginning was the Word, and the Word was with God, and the Word was God.*

"Oh," Helen gasped and then unleashed the tears of eight decades of life as the truth rose within her like the tide.

"Mom. Mom! What is it? What's happened? Are you all right? What is all this? Why are you crying? Mom?" Kat swept into the room with Paul right behind her, looking at his phone.

He put a hand on Kat's shoulder. "Kat. There's a report on the news that an American base has been attacked in Afghanistan."

"It's Nathan." Helen sobbed. "He called. It's his unit, I know it. He called and now-now-oh!" Helen saw a dark tunnel and a small light that lingered for a moment before even that light was gone.

# Chapter Seventeen

"She's coming around," Kat's voice.

"Helen? Can you hear me?" Paul's voice. A strong hand gripping her wrist between thumb and forefingers.

"Charles?"

"Helen. It's Paul. You're all right. You've just worn yourself out. Take a sip of water."

Water. Cool on her lips, her tongue. Her dry throat. So thirsty.

"Mom? How many Irish coffees have you had?" Kat's voice.

Helen opened her eyes seeing Kat through fluttering eyelids. Sniffing her coffee cup. Eyeing the whiskey bottle.

"Two. Just two. What time is it?" She adjusted herself in the overstuffed chair. Tried to sit up higher.

"Eleven. Keep sipping the water, Helen," Paul continued to monitor her pulse.

"You're sure I shouldn't call the ambulance?" Kat asked.

"She's fine," He winked at Helen. "Just overworking herself as usual from the looks of it."

Kat collected pages from the manuscript. "Mom, have you taken on an editing project? I didn't know you were still accepting work. This one appears to have needed quite an overhaul."

Helen took a long draft of the water. "Where's Harry?"

Paul shrugged. "We parted ways at the church. Said he had something he had to take care of before tomorrow."

Kat noticed the Bible open on the desk. "What's this? Mom? Have you been reading the Bible? Was this Dad's?"

"It was a gift. Delivered tonight, after you left, in that box." Helen indicated the empty gift box. "It's rigged somehow, electronically, to that computer gizmo. I'm guessing it's Harry's doing."

"Rigged? What do you mean rigged?" asked Paul.

"The pages turn by themselves and verses light up, then that computer plays scenes, videos, from my life. It even had a recording of the night I was born. I can't imagine where Harry found that. That's why I have to talk with him."

Kat and Paul exchanged glances, then looked back at her.

"Explain that again, Helen?" Paul had that doctor look now. Helen was all too familiar with the furrowed eyebrows of concern.

"Well, don't look at me like I'm crazy. It must be one of Harry's schemes to make me think about Jesus and ... and it almost worked."

"What do you mean, almost?" Kat sat on the arm of the davenport next to the overstuffed chair until Helen raised her eyebrows and she sat properly on the seat cushion.

"Nothing. Not nothing, exactly, but—I don't know. Some of the Bible verses and the scenes of my life made me introspective. Christmas Eve and all. I ... I almost want to believe, but then I received the call from Nathan and—" She welled up again. "I can't bear to lose another boy, Katherine. I can't bear it. I want to believe in Jesus to keep Nathan safe, I even prayed for him tonight ..."

160

"You prayed, Mom?"

"Yes, yes, I probably did it all wrong and there's no reason why he should do anything for me but I did ask him to keep our boy safe. You and Paul, though, your prayers are the ones that will count. You're both so exactly what he wants, I know he'll answer your prayers. We've nothing to worry about. Nathan will come through this alive because of you, right?"

Paul looked at the floor then stood. "I'm going to get my bag. I'll be back."

Kat moved from the davenport to sit beside Helen. She took Helen's hand in hers and for once, Helen didn't pull away. "Mom, I don't believe that loving Jesus in any way guarantees that Nathan will be kept safe."

"You don't?"

She shook her head. "I pray for it, of course, like mothers have always prayed when they send their sons to war—or anywhere for that matter. We live in a world full of wars and every child grows up on the front line of some battle. There are worse ways to lose a child than to death. But my prayers are requests, not incantations or magic spells."

"Then what good is it to pray? To follow your religion? To have faith?"

Kat studied her face. "You're really asking those questions, aren't you? Mom, I've trusted my entire life to Christ. I tell him daily what I want. Of course, I want my children to be healthy and safe and to love him. I raise them according to Biblical principles. I intercede for them in prayer. But I know that God sometimes calls us to bear hard things; to suffer for purposes we can't always see. His plan for Nathan may be for him to lay down his life for our country."

"Are you saying you'll be fine if Nathan is one of those casualties?"

Kat swallowed. "If Nathan is one of those casualties, it will tear me apart. I'll feel that loss as hard as the one you felt when we lost CJ, but God will be beside me and he will walk me through the valley of the shadow of death. Nathan loves Jesus and I know that one day, we'll be together forever."

Helen bit her lower lip, thinking. "But if what you believe is true and I choose to follow Jesus, I'll never see CJ again. I want to see him. I want to go where he is. What if I make the wrong choice?"

Kat stroked Helen's hand. "I don't know where CJ is now, Mom. He did come to believe in a higher power through some of his twelve-step groups. Maybe somewhere in there he came to have faith in Christ but if he didn't, you won't do him any good to follow him to hell. There's no comfort there, Mom. Not even from a mother's presence or a son's face. You can't imagine that would be the right choice. And I promise you, if he is there, it will only bring him more pain if you join him."

Helen turned her face away, but Kat placed her hand on her cheek and turned her gaze back toward Kat. "Think about it, Mom. CJ loved you. Wherever he is now, he knows the truth. If life ends completely, then this doesn't matter. But if the Bible is right and there is a heaven and a hell, CJ would want you to be with God as much as I do."

"I wish I could believe that." Helen looked over at the Bible on the desk and paused.

"What is it, Mom?" Kat asked, looking in the same direction.

"I ... well, this is when the pages would normally start to turn and there would be a verse that lights up and ..." She sighed. Had she imagined everything?

Kat walked over to the Bible and turned, expertly, to a page near the last third of the book. "I don't doubt that something supernatural has taken place here tonight, Mom. I could tell you amazing stories of what Paul and I have seen through the years. I know you love words and there are none more powerful than the very words of God. This story in Luke might help you understand what I'm saying about joining loved ones in the afterlife."

Paul came in and sat so he could listen to Helen's heart and take her blood pressure. Kat continued to collect the pages of Helen's story. "Mom? Wait. What is this? Is this your own project? Something you've written?"

"Put it down. Put it down right now. I'll clean it up." Helen pushed Paul aside and wriggled her way to the edge of the overstuffed chair, placing her feet on the floor and looking around for her cane.

"And, she's back," Paul declared as he stood. Placing the stethoscope around his neck, he kissed Kat on the cheek. "I'm going to check on the girls and see if I can reach Nathan."

Kat nodded and they exchanged a long glance before he left. She laid the pages she'd gathered on the desk and watched as Helen hobbled around snatching up the others.

"What are you staring at?" Helen snapped. "I'm fine. Just a combination of too much nostalgia and not enough water to offset the Irish coffee."

Kat's voice was quiet. "What happened in here tonight, Mom?"

"Someone made a fool of an old woman. That's what happened. And when I find out who, they'll get a piece of my mind."

"Let me help you." Kat reached for a page, but Helen stuck her cane on the paper.

"Leave it, I said. Leave it. I'm going to clean it all up myself and have a moment's peace before I go to bed. I'm fine." Helen heard the sharpness in her own voice as she had hundreds of times before but this time she felt something different at the sound. Sadness. Regret. Remorse.

"I'll go see what Paul has learned, but I'll look in on you before we go to bed."

"I'm not an invalid, Katherine. I can take care of myself." She consciously tried to soften her tone. "But, I do want to know the minute you have word on our boy."

Katherine closed the study door behind her. Solitude had always been her refuge. Right now, it felt more like having fallen down a rabbit hole hearing nothing but the scurry of moles and the pounding of her own heart.

"What is happening to me?" she said aloud. She picked up the Dickens she'd intended to read tonight. "Well, you'd understand me, wouldn't you, Ebenezer?"

Somehow the name sparked an aural memory from her childhood. At least, she thought it was a memory, until she noticed the tablet glowing again, voices singing an old, familiar hymn. As she walked closer, she placed a hand over her heart at the sight of herself, a little girl in braids, standing between AJ and her father during Sunday morning service. Her father's beautiful tenor voice belting out the words, "Here I raise mine Ebenezer, hither by thine help I'm come. And I hope by thy good pleasure safely to arrive at home. Jesus sought me when a stranger, wandering from the fold of God. He to rescue me from danger interposed His precious blood."

She grabbed at the tablet as the music faded, longing for a lasting glimpse of her father, the sound of his voice, the comfort of his knowing presence. "Please," she pleaded with the screen. "Please, just one more verse."

The Bible glowed where Kat had left it open and Helen leaned forward to read the story of Lazarus and the rich man. The rich man was pleading from his place in hell for Lazarus to send someone to his family to get word that they should make choices to avoid the torment he endured.

When she finished reading, she looked out into the darkness one more time. It was too dark to see the waves but here and there, lights glinted off them. And the boat still had its sail lights forming a Christmas tree with a star blinking at the top.

Suddenly, Helen felt a relief, a peace she'd never before known that coursed through her veins like a more powerful elixir than is known to exist on earth. She smiled at the boat and then at her own reflection as the blinking star glowed in the place where her heart beat strong and faster now that she had made her choice.

"I want to live," she said to her reflection.

She nodded and turned to the Bible. "I choose life. I want to live!"

And all at once, she wanted to be with her family, sit with them, usher in the holiday seeing their faces, sharing their laughter, drinking in their love. The clock on her shelf chimed the hour. It was here. Christmas was upon her household.

Helen snatched up her shawl and cane and made her way carefully down the stairs, into the darkened foyer, hoping, praying the others were still up sharing a warm mug and cookies in the parlor. But as she reached the bottom stair, she froze and held her breath.

A shadow, now two, filled the windows on either side of the door. The outside lights were out as they were in the adjacent rooms. The sound of scraping. Gruff whispers. Someone trying to break in.

"Paul. Paul." Her mind formed the word and her mouth tried to call out, but all she could manage was a choked whisper as her throat filled with fear. No. No. This couldn't be. She couldn't let them destroy this night. This first night. This first moment of her knowing the truth at last.

And her family, the girls, if this was a home invasion, what would become of the girls? The doorknob rattled. Helen tried to think. "Do something. Do something," she said. "God help me." She prayed

165

as she took her cane in one hand like a club and grabbed a pointed umbrella from the stand beside the door with the other.

She tried again, to call Paul, but she still had no voice so she braced herself and readied her weapons just as the door jolted from its secure lock and swung open. At last, she found her voice and screamed as she lunged at the two intruders in the darkened foyer. Wildly she swung her cane, catching one on the shoulder but her finger triggered the mechanism on the umbrella so that it opened up like a canvas shield and she found herself futilely thrusting it at the other intruder's mid-section.

The two invaders yelled holding up their arms, and crying out, but it wasn't until the rest of the family was upon them and someone switched on the light she realized they were calling "Gran. Gran, it's us! Stop! Gran!"

"Harry? Harry, what are you—Nathan! Oh, Nathan!" Helen dropped her arsenal and flung herself at Nathan, who was standing there in uniform rubbing the shoulder she'd battered with her cane.

Everyone talked at once, asking questions, checking Nathan and Harry for injuries, laughing at the image of Helen wielding the umbrella like a shield. Finally, Nathan held up a hand to quiet everyone so he could explain.

"I'm sorry I worried you all. The timing of that assault on the base in Afghanistan was just a terrible coincidence. I've been praying all day for those troops and their families. But I received a last minute furlough and decided to surprise you all; only Harry knew."

Helen scowled at him. "Why did you call me earlier if you knew you were on your way home?"

"Well, my flight out of New Jersey was delayed and then canceled. I worried that I wouldn't be able to find another flight home or that I'd be traveling when our Skype call was scheduled. Fortunately, I got a last minute standby and was able to text Harry to pick me up."

Kat, by now, was clinging to Nathan and couldn't be persuaded to let him go. "Have you eaten?"

"Not a thing since breakfast. I kept thinking I'd make it here in time for a meal." He replied.

"That settles it. Everyone to the kitchen for Christmas pancakes!" she declared.

"At midnight?" Paul laughed.

"Why not! I don't feel like sleeping—anyone else?" Kat said as she grabbed Nathan's arm and escorted him toward the kitchen.

As the others left, Helen motioned for Harry to stay back with her in the foyer.

"What's up, Gran? You had me pretty worried earlier tonight," he said.

"Tonight is a long story, my boy, and I'll be happy to give you the details tomorrow. All that's important for you to know right now is that I finally understand."

"Understand what, Gran?"

"What this day is all about. What you and your mother and your grandfather have been praying I would understand for years."

"Gran, are you saying you believe in Jesus?"

She nodded, caught off guard by the well of emotion that kept her from saying the words aloud.

Harry picked her up and spun around. "Gran, that's amazing! Absolutely amazing! We have to tell the others."

"No, no. Not just yet. This is Nathan's moment. There will be plenty of time to share the news tomorrow. I just had to let you know, my precious boy. Thank you for never giving up on a stubborn old woman."

"I love you, Gran."

"I love you too, Harry."

"Hey!" Paul stuck his head out of the hallway that led to the kitchen. "You two are missing out on Christmas pancakes!"

"Oh, no, we're not. Make sure I get a double batch! Try to remember that I'm the one who delivered the Golden Boy to your door." Harry laughed as he and Helen headed down the hall.

"Yeah, yeah. What's your name again?" Paul teased.

Helen joined them in the warm, shining kitchen and ate three pancakes herself as she drank in the laughter and love of her persistent, faithful family.

# Chapter Eighteen

When dawn arrived on Christmas day, Harry woke everyone early as was his tradition. Banging on doors, he called them all out to open stockings beneath the tree.

"Are you kidding me?" hollered Nathan. "We only went to bed five minutes ago."

"Tradition is tradition, Golden Boy," Harry said as he banged on his sisters' bedroom door.

"Fine. We're coming but one of these years we're sleeping in, Harry," Cara called.

"Not this year. This year is special," he proclaimed.

"What's so special about this year besides Nathan being home?" Kat asked as she kissed his cheek and yawned, straightening her bed-head with her fingers.

"You'll see. Gran and I have a surprise." He winked as she passed.

"I'm not sure I can handle more surprises this year," she said. "I'm sure I can't without a cup of coffee. I'll meet you downstairs. Your father will be out in a moment."

Harry knocked on Helen's bedroom door. No response. He knocked again and opened the door a crack, then wider as he realized she hadn't been to bed.

"Gran?" He checked her private bathroom but then headed to her study. Sometimes she fell asleep in there when she'd been reading late at night.

"Knock, knock. Christmas morning! Time for stockings!" Harry opened the door to her study. Sure enough. She was asleep on the overstuffed chair.

"That's it, Gran. I never thought I'd live to see the day when you were the last one up in the morning! Time to get a move on. It's Christmas after all." He leaned over to kiss her forehead and then stopped.

Something was wrong.

Harry watched Helen's chest, waiting for the rise and fall of her sleeping breath.

Nothing.

He squatted beside her chair and touched a hand to her arm but snatched it away when he felt nothing but cold.

"Harry?" Paul came to the doorway holding two ties. "Which one do you think—"

"Dad?" The quiver in Harry's voice must have startled Paul. He looked up from the ties and studied Helen with a practiced eye.

"Harry, son." His voice was soft as he stepped into the room and closed the door. Silently, he walked to Helen and touched a hand to her wrist, then to her neck. "Oh, Helen."

Harry stood up and turned away to look out at the sky just beginning to glow. He looked down at the desk and saw his tablet lying atop an old Bible. Beside them, a neatly stacked manuscript tied with a red bow and a tag that read, "To Harry, who never gave up on a stubborn old soul." On the other side of the manuscript was a fancy red pen in an even fancier box and a note written on yellowed parchment. Harry would have to read it later because his eyes, just now, swam with tears.

"Son, I'm so sorry. I know how special she was to you. I'm so sorry for you to find her this way." Paul laid a hand on Harry's shoulder and Harry nodded.

"I'm all right, Dad. I'm actually way more than all right."

"What do you mean?"

"She gave me my Christmas gift last night and it's one that will last forever."

Later that day, as everyone busied themselves with their gifts or with arrangements for Helen, Harry scanned the pages of her life story. As he did with every book, he turned immediately to the end.

He was fascinated to find that the typewritten pages ended with a solid blot of red ink that filled one-third of what must have been the original final page. After that, though, Helen penned her last thoughts in the hours between their midnight pancakes and dawn.

Harry was enrapt as over several pages she told of the mysterious package she'd received and the events alone in her room thereafter. All the while he was reading, he shook his head or hmphed as Helen shared the process that transpired as she spent Christmas Eve alone with just a Bible and, apparently, the Holy Spirit.

At last, he read her final paragraph aloud to the others.

"Little did I realize when I began to write my life story that I would end with the telling of my birth—my rebirth, of course, but still, the start of an eternal future. There were times as God walked me through the final edit of my life that I was sure he intended to destroy me by showing me how desperately I had failed. In the last hours, however, I have come to see that his intent was not to show me my failure but to reveal his presence throughout all my days. Decades before this night when I, at last, chose life with Christ, he had already chosen life with me. He has been there from my start and he will be there when I take my final breath this side of the veil.

"The Bible showed me one final passage tonight before I lay down to rest up for the coming morning (I know Harry will be knocking early). As I read it, I remembered it was the passage that Charles chose as his "life verse" for his baptism. At the time, I recall that I scoffed at him, but now, I stand with him in claiming this as my life verse as well. When the holidays are through, we'll see if anyone is brave enough to baptize this old, ornery soul. Until then, I will claim these words from Philippians 1:19-21 as my testimony: *for I know that through your prayers and God's provision of the Spirit of Jesus Christ what has happened to me will turn out for my deliverance. I eagerly expect and hope that I will in no way be ashamed, but will have sufficient courage so that now as always Christ will be exalted in my body, whether by life or by death. For to me, to live is Christ and to die is gain.*

"I expect I will spend eternity thanking God for waiting for me and thanking my loved ones for never giving up in prayer, in witness, and in stubbornly confronting me with the truth. Know that it all came together for me one magical Christmas Eve when God called me out on my own words and gave me, instead, the words of life.

"I'll hand it to the Almighty. It's hard to surprise an old broad like me, but he pulled it off. I can only imagine what surprises he has in store for the future.

"Merry Christmas, Harry. I'm looking forward to our big adventure."

Harry smiled. "So am I, Gran. So am I."

# Discussion Starters for Red Pen Redemption

1. In the first decade of Helen's life, she experienced a significant loss that affected her understanding of God. What early experiences with God affected the way you see Him? Did anything change that?

2. How could it help you to know what early experiences affected the way others think about God?

3. In her second decade of life, Helen's worldview was strongly affected by others—the boys at school, her stepmother, and Monty. Who influenced you during your adolescence? How did that impact your life?

4. In chapter six, Helen says this, "I've lived with purpose. I've worked hard. I won't let you stain it all red just because I didn't mutter a few words that made your Son my personal Savior. That's crazy." She gestured as though God was sitting in the room. "You're going to judge every word? No one can stand up to that scrutiny. If that's your standard, then no one deserves heaven!" What's your response to her reaction? Can you understand it? What would be your answer if she said it to you?

5. To which character do you most easily relate in this story? Who is hardest for you to understand, to like? Do any of them remind you of people in your life? How?

6. Kat became a Christian as a teen-ager in the seventies and her family didn't understand or welcome her transformation. If you're a Christian, what was the response of your loved ones when you became one? If you're not a Christian, do you understand why Helen reacted to Kat the way she did? Why?

7. How did the times in which she lived affect Helen's life choices? What is it about the times in which you live that most affect your choices?

8. In chapter eight, Helen's choice had a negative effect on Season but she learns that God worked good out of that situation for Season. She argues that should bless her negative actions. What would you say to Helen about that? What good has God brought from bad in your life?

9. In the decades of "The Black Hole," Helen endured terrible struggles and suffered a serious depression that affected how she treated others. How have you responded to the trials you've faced and how has that affected those around you?

10. Why do you think Helen's grandson, Harry, is able to reach Helen when others aren't?

11. In chapter seventeen, Helen reveals her fear of making a choice that will separate her forever from CJ. Can you relate to her fear? How does Kat respond to her? How would her response affect you?

12. Does this story have a happy ending? Why or why not? If you were the author of Red Pen Redemption, would Helen Bancroft live or die at the end of the story? Why? If Helen had lived longer, what do you imagine her life would look like for the next year?